PENGUIN
THE PREMIER M

Dr Geeta Sundar did her schooling from St Joseph's Convent, Jabalpur, and her bachelor's and postgraduation in medicine from Netaji Subhash Chandra Bose Medical College, Jabalpur.

She began her practice as a consultant in medicine at BL Kapoor Memorial Hospital, Delhi. Currently she has a consultancy practice at Bibvewadi, Pune, and is also an online health counsel for a leading insurance brokerage firm.

Several of her articles on health have appeared in national magazines and newspapers like *Femina*, the *Times of India* and the *Indian Express*. She began her career as a writer seven years ago and has published a number of books on health-related issues.

She has followed the game of cricket and enjoyed it since childhood. It was natural then that when she started writing her first fiction, cricket automatically crept into it!

Dr Geeta Sundar lives in Pune.

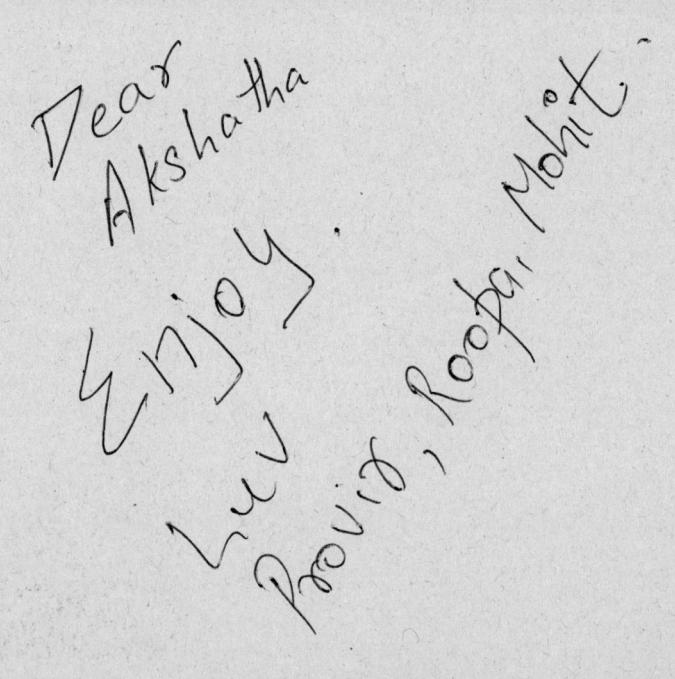

The Premier Murder League

Geeta Sundar

PENGUIN BOOKS

PENGUIN BOOKS
Published by the Penguin Group
Penguin Books India Pvt. Ltd, 11 Community Centre, Panchsheel Park,
New Delhi 110 017, India
Penguin Group (USA) Inc., 375 Hudson Street, New York, New York 10014, USA
Penguin Group (Canada), 90 Eglinton Avenue East, Suite 700, Toronto,
Ontario, M4P 2Y3, Canada (a division of Pearson Penguin Canada Inc.)
Penguin Books Ltd, 80 Strand, London WC2R 0RL, England
Penguin Ireland, 25 St Stephen's Green, Dublin 2, Ireland
(a division of Penguin Books Ltd)
Penguin Group (Australia), 250 Camberwell Road, Camberwell,
Victoria 3124, Australia (a division of Pearson Australia Group Pty Ltd)
Penguin Group (NZ), 67 Apollo Drive, Rosedale, North Shore 0632,
New Zealand (a division of Pearson New Zealand Ltd)
Penguin Group (South Africa) (Pty) Ltd, 24 Sturdee Avenue, Rosebank,
Johannesburg 2196, South Africa

Penguin Books Ltd, Registered Offices: 80 Strand, London WC2R 0RL, England

First published by Penguin Books India 2010

Copyright © Geeta Sundar 2010

All rights reserved

10 9 8 7 6 5 4 3 2 1

This is a work of fiction. Names, characters, places and incidents are either the product of the author's imagination or are used fictitiously and any resemblance to any actual person, living or dead, events or locales is entirely coincidental.

ISBN 9780143067825

Typeset in Bembo Roman by SŪRYA, New Delhi
Printed at Manipal Press Ltd, Manipal

This book is sold subject to the condition that it shall not, by way of trade or otherwise, be lent, resold, hired out, or otherwise circulated without the publisher's prior written consent in any form of binding or cover other than that in which it is published and without a similar condition including this condition being imposed on the subsequent purchaser and without limiting the rights under copyright reserved above, no part of this publication may be reproduced, stored in or introduced into a retrieval system, or transmitted in any form or by any means (electronic, mechanical, photocopying, recording or otherwise), without the prior written permission of both the copyright owner and the above-mentioned publisher of this book.

*This book is dedicated to my beloved father who
passed away recently;
To Sachin Tendulkar for many an exciting moment;
And also to the three cricketers I admire wholeheartedly—
Kapil Dev and M.S. Dhoni for their down-to-earth sincerity,
talent and confidence;
Rahul Dravid for holding fort so many times in his career with
perfect technique and sheer determination.*

Prologue

● September 2007

It was raining heavily in Delhi that night. S.N. Rao, the minister for sports, was chewing two paans after his dinner as he prepared to go to bed. He was in his farmhouse located at a very picturesque, though isolated, spot forty kilometres from the city. It had been a long day but a fruitful one in the end, since the counselling session with his son had gone off well. He had shared the good news with his wife Indu. She was currently in the US, visiting her sister who was recovering from a surgery for breast cancer. He thought fondly about his wife. His lovely wife, who even at fifty could give the current beauty queens a run for their money, whose flawless complexion and chiselled features owed nothing to beauty parlours or plastic surgery. The only embellishment she needed on her face was a dark maroon bindi.

Suddenly he was flooded with her scent, a heady combination of jasmine and chandan that at this age too set his pulse racing. Their life together had been a good one. Thinking about her even for a few moments filled him with happiness and a feeling of being blessed. He missed her badly but comforted himself that she would be back with him soon.

His mind switched back to the paans he was chewing, they tasted unusually sweet. The paanwala had probably put too much gulkand, the sugary rose mixture, in it, he thought. A little while later there was a strong burning sensation in his throat as if somebody had set it on fire. Then suddenly he started retching violently but nothing came out. He went to the bathroom where he managed to throw up.

There was a sense of relief since he had got rid of his nausea, but this was short-lived. The discomfort in his stomach grew again till there were three more bouts of vomiting. By now he was wheezing and panting and there were severe cramps in his stomach followed by diarrhoea.

He came out of the bathroom and scrambled in his bedside drawer for his medicines. He pulled out his inhaler, took a puff and spotted an anti-diarrhoeal too. His hands began to shake as he poured himself water and swallowed the medicine—but he got no relief.

I must tell Vineet, he thought, remembering his son was at home. He looked at the door to his bedroom which was closed because of the air conditioner running. It suddenly seemed a long distance away. Wheezing slightly and walking slowly because of the weakness, he reached to open the door but could not. It seemed to have been locked from outside! Then he went back looking for his mobile to call his son, but was not able to find it either. What the hell is happening? He was panicking now. Something was seriously wrong!

After another visit to the bathroom he decided he would shout for help. But only a hoarse cry emerged from his parched throat. He inched to the door again. In his desperation, he tried to bang on it but nobody seemed to hear him. Probably his blows were feeble. By now he was losing his strength and breathing heavily. He was so weak that he was unable to stand and only able to crawl, that too with great difficulty. He felt as if his muscles were made of lead, but he was aware of what was happening to him since his mind was remarkably clear.

He was sure now that the paans had contained something, he should have spat them out immediately. But it was too late. The person who had done this to him had been clever enough to take his mobile away and also bolt the door from outside. He was lying on the ground—writhing and thinking, desperate to try something. Anything! Then he did the only thing he could. Shakily, he pulled out a pen from his pocket and used it to leave a message on the wall.

Exhausted by the effort and the knowledge that the end was near, he lay down flat on the floor in shavasana, the corpse pose, and softly started chanting 'Hare Krishna, Hare Rama' between long and deep laboured breaths. His body began to jerk as he suffered a fit. To his horror he felt totally paralysed. Oh God, I'm going to die! he thought.

He passed away after four hours.

Silence descended as his struggle ended. The door stood like a silent witness—it was now unlocked!

One

Just as Ravi Sharma, the deputy commissioner of police of the crime branch, walked briskly into his office at the police headquarters, he received a call. It was the commissioner of police on the other side, 'Ravi, can you come to my office immediately; Mr S.N. Rao, the union minister for sports, passed away last night at his farmhouse.'

As he waited for his junior, Commissioner Bedi thanked his stars that he had a DCP like Ravi working under him, who had solved more criminal cases in the last five years than anyone else in the department. He smiled as Ravi entered and pointed to the chair in front. 'Hope you enjoyed the well-deserved break with your parents. Have they gone back?'

'Yes sir, they've gone back to my brother,' Ravi replied saluting and then took the seat before his senior. Ravi was a tall, dark, good-looking police officer with a no-nonsense demeanour that added to his appeal.

'Well, coming to S.N. Rao's death, most probably it is a natural one, but given his status as union minister for sports and his status as a cricket board member, it is better to be sure. We don't want to find out later that the death was unnatural and miss out on vital evidence. Remember this had happened with the foreign minister three years back and there was a big hue and cry?'

Ravi nodded. 'Yes sir.'

His senior continued, 'I want you and Rahul to go to the farmhouse where he died and carry out a spot inspection. I know I could send someone junior with you, but I'm afraid he might miss crucial evidence, if there is any. Go through the place thoroughly, talk to everyone there and find out exactly what happened. I'll await your report in the evening.'

Ravi saluted and left the room. CP Bedi called up the home minister. 'Sir, I've put my best man on the job. You can rest assured that if there's even a hint of foul play, he'll find out. You can tell the Prime Minister that.'

'Thank you, Commissioner Bedi. Rao was a good man and was very close to the PM. The PM is concerned that the death was sudden and at a place where medical attention could not reach him quickly. He also feels that since the elections are nearing, anything can happen. Er . . . you get my point?'

'Don't worry sir, I'll report back to you in the evening.'

~

Ravi went to his office and called the assistant commissioner of police and his junior, Rahul Singh. 'I am on my way, be with you in five minutes!' Rahul Singh was young, dashing and very outgoing. Since college he had been interested in criminal investigation and had read many books on the subject. Joining the Indian Police Service had been a natural choice for him. He had a keen mind and even though he was still junior he was growing continuously on the job. One more trait he had was to unquestioningly follow what his boss Ravi asked of him. It was only under Ravi that he had started to grasp the practical nuances of his profession and learnt how to solve crimes in the shortest possible time.

Rahul and Ravi had become so close professionally that they seemed to operate on the same wavelength, often understanding each other without a word having been spoken.

Rahul had barely entered Ravi's office that the latter got up briskly and said, 'Let's go, I'll explain things on the way.' As they started walking down the long corridor, Ravi began, 'Commissioner sahib called me just now and told me that the union minister for sports, S.N. Rao has passed away at his farmhouse. He wants us to go there and do a spot inspection just to be certain that there was no foul play. I have called up the intelligence guys and told them to keep a printout of what they have on him. We'll pick it up and go through it in the jeep on our way to the farmhouse. I've asked Constable Hassan to drive us there.'

Rahul smiled to himself: so typical of his senior. He hadn't wasted any time. He was very fond of Ravi and felt he knew him inside out. Ravi had an arresting personality and the piercing eyes of a policeman that did not miss much. His parents lived in the US with his brother and he had no close relatives in Delhi. Rahul knew that besides being a colleague and a junior officer, he was also his boss's friend, and more importantly, a sounding board for his ideas.

They picked up the intelligence report on Rao and got into Ravi's official jeep which the loyal Hassan had kept ready near the exit. As they drove to the farmhouse, Rahul read out the report, "'Dr S.N. Rao was born to a wealthy farmer fifty-six years back in Andhra Pradesh. He was educated at his village school and then went to the Agricultural College in Hyderabad from where he did his graduation, master's, and then followed it up with a doctorate. But before S.N. Rao could implement the knowledge he had gained in the Agricultural College, he had joined politics and soon became so involved in it that farming took a back seat.'"

'So he earned his doctorate—it was not the type that is "conferred" on most politicians by some university that needs patronage!' Ravi exclaimed in surprise.

'Yes chief, and that's why he probably had that erudite look to him. Let me read on.

'"S.N. Rao rose very rapidly in his political career. By the time he was forty, he was already a minister at the state level. Television was in a nascent stage then and he got the lucky break of starting a TV channel. He called it 'Indus' and within a decade, he had a full-fledged multilingual TV channel, most of the programmes of which had very high TRP ratings. S.N. Rao was by now very rich and powerful, since he was also a minister at the centre. As most of his activities were now in Delhi, he decided to shift there and built himself a big house."'

'Rahul, prior to reading this report, I knew only two things about him. First that he was considered a capable administrator and second that his daughter is married to Dilip Singh, the famous cricketer. I'd met Dilip once on a flight. Despite being a celebrity, he is a very warm and approachable person.'

'That's why the whole nation still loves him so much, chief. Hm! Let me see what else is there . . . "S.N. Rao married early and his wife Indu also came from a rich family. Indu's father was a very big landowner and farmer from Andhra Pradesh.

'"S.N. Rao has two sons and two daughters, all helping in the family business. The children had chosen to study business and finance so that they could help in the running of their channel. Dilip Singh, the famous cricketer, is married to his daughter Anu.

'"S.N. Rao had been heading his state cricket board and about two years back, had got elected to the national cricket board." Well those are the facts about Rao, but there is also a character report attached: "S.N. Rao is an unusual businessman and an uncommon politician. He is actually known and admired for his ethical practices. As a politician he is shrewd but always toes the party line. He'll pay the occasional bribe but never goes beyond that. The only negative factor in his life is his eldest son Vineet—the black sheep of the family. Vineet is chronically in debt and has every kind of bad habit that can be acquired, including gambling and keeping a mistress."'

Rahul smiled. 'Rao seems to be an amazing person, chief. He actually rose up to become a cabinet minister, that too, ethically!'

Ravi spoke thoughtfully, 'Yes. A rare breed indeed; that's why the Prime Minister is so concerned at his death. Let's see what we can find out. Somehow I have a bad feeling about all this.'

Rahul and Ravi could not possibly have known at the time that the minister's death was only the tip of the iceberg . . .

Two

It took DCP Ravi and ACP Rahul more than forty minutes to reach S.N. Rao's farmhouse. The security guard at the gate hastily unlocked it as soon as he saw the uniformed men in the jeep.

'Lovely, isn't it? It looks so peaceful and serene, it seems unlikely that any crime could have been committed here,' said Rahul as Hassan drove the jeep in.

'We are here to look around the place,' Ravi told the caretaker who had come out of the house on hearing the sound of an approaching jeep. The caretaker nodded.

Before going in Ravi took Hassan aside, 'Bring the security guard to the living room and keep both the farmhouse employees under your observation. Also find out if there is anyone else and round them up.'

'Yes sir!' Hassan saluted smartly in response. He loved being a part of the investigation.

The rooms were locked, so Ravi asked the caretaker to open the doors and take them around. 'Rahul, you check out the son's bedroom while I go through Rao's,' he instructed. Ravi entered the master bedroom that was neat and tidy. The caretaker had already cleaned up the place!

Most of the evidence would have been lost even if it was there to be found, Ravi thought. But he looked around hoping that there would still be something left to salvage. He examined the room inch by inch leaving out nothing. There was a faint smell of vomit that pervaded the air. He had switched on all the lights and was also carrying a powerful magnifying glass, a camera, and had asked the caretaker for a broom to sweep under the bed. Normally this would have been done by a team, but since this case was sensitive, Ravi chose not to have too many people as part of the investigation. He knew Rahul, who was similarly equipped to examine the other room, was quite capable of handling things himself too. The bed and floor were clean, so was the bathroom and the rest of the furniture. Ravi now went over the walls, first while standing and then sitting on his haunches to cover the lower parts, but found nothing. Then he decided to go over the floor and walls again. His instinct told him there was something there.

As he reached for the wall near the door for the second time, he suddenly became alert. He lay down on the floor—yes, there was something scrawled on the wall! It could be the handiwork of a child done long back. But the message, although an untidy scrawl as if made with difficulty, was certainly no childish prank. It clearly read: 'cellphone taken, door locked'. Only Rao could have written that! Even a veteran police officer like Ravi was excited. He took out the camera and took a picture of the message—

Cell Phone taken door locked

He combed the room again and came out. Then he went to see how Rahul was doing.

His junior was almost finished with his investigation as Ravi entered, showing him a thumbs down to indicate he had found nothing. Ravi flashed a smile and gave a thumbs up sign in response. Rahul was excited. Together they went back to Rao's bedroom.

'Tell me, can you smell something Rahul?' Ravi asked.

'I get a mild smell of vomit,' Rahul answered, sniffing for more underlying scents.

'Right, that makes me suspect some kind of poison may have been used on Rao.'

'But chief, vomiting can also occur in other cases, like a severe heart attack due to intense pain.'

Ravi smiled. Rahul missed nothing. 'Agreed Rahul, but we are trained to have a high index of suspicion that takes nothing for granted. If you are in a crowd and someone calls out your name, you will not be wrong in thinking that someone is calling you. But you cannot take it for granted, since there could be other Rahuls in the crowd.'

'Right, chief!'

'Well, my suspicions having been aroused, I examined the room in detail and look what I found,' Ravi pointed to the wall near the bathroom. 'Look at the lower part of the wall there and tell me what you see.'

Rahul took a few steps, bent down and saw the scrawled message.

'What does this mean chief? Has there been some foul play? Did someone try to kill Rao and was he prevented from escaping or calling anybody for help. Was he left to die?'

'Probably, and he left this message before passing away. So we have some grounds for suspecting that Rao did not die a natural death. We continue to work on all possibilities until they are ruled out due to some other positive evidence.'

There was a glint of admiration for his chief in Rahul's eyes.

'Now let's see what the rest of the house and the farm reveal, and especially what we can get out of the two employees, Rahul. We will first go over the grounds and the farm and then question these two. If they have something to hide, it will be good to test their patience a bit.'

Ravi asked Hassan to seal the bedrooms, keep the keys with him and to continue to watch the two employees. Then they walked towards the farm.

Since it was the rainy season, the grounds looked green and freshly washed. The farm was a 100-acre area with an artificial lake, undulating slopes and hillocks, peppered with fruit trees. The area around the house had lawns and flowers, but the rest of the land resembled a natural jungle. There was a walkway through this jungle that ran up to the lake, and Rao had built a small temple there atop a hillock, where the two detectives were now heading.

Some scattered farmhands working under the fruit trees stopped their activities in consternation and followed the police officers with their eyes till they disappeared.

When they reached the temple, Rahul took off his shoes and socks and entered inside. 'Come sir, let's pray for the success of our visit.'

'Rahul, I hardly ever go to religious places. I have only one idol, and that is Mahatma Gandhi, whom I admire for the strength of his convictions and also for the unconventional, but highly effective methods he employed to solve problems confronting the nation.'

'I know chief, you carry his laminated photo in your wallet, and I've seen the amazing collection of Gandhiji's books at your residence. I wouldn't be surprised if it is the largest private collection of the Mahatma's works outside his family in the world.'

'I wouldn't be too sure about that, but I am not an atheist. It's just that I visit temples only when my parents come over. I have a soft corner for Shirdi Sai baba who, according to me, was the closest to a saint that a person could get. I respect him for the fact that he treated people of all communities alike and is revered by everyone.' He smiled at Rahul, took off his shoes and socks and went in.

It was a tiny temple but had a very peaceful ambience. Both the officers bowed before the deities and then came out.

'I wonder chief what the minister would have asked of God had he known it was his last visit to the temple.'

Ravi was suddenly impatient, 'Let's go back to the house, Rahul; I get the feeling there will be more evidence to find there.'

They went back and found Hassan dutifully guarding the two employees.

'Rahul, there seem to be only two employees in the house. Question the security guard and I'll do the same with the caretaker. Since we're suspecting that some kind of poison was administered to Rao, remember to ask whether paan or alcohol were served. These are the best vehicles for poisoning. They can be given to the person at night after dinner and the assailant can walk out, leaving the victim to die.'

Ravi questioned Subba Rao the caretaker regarding S.N. Rao's visit and asked him to describe it from the beginning till the body was discovered.

'Sir, I'm still in a state of shock at bade sahib's death. I've been with him for twenty years and had followed him to Delhi from Hyderabad along with his doctor and driver. For all of us it is a loss we can hardly bear. I'm also concerned about seeing the police here. Are you suspecting that his death was not a natural one?' He looked agitated at the thought.

'My dear man, your master was a very important person, so we have to be absolutely certain that his death was natural. We are here just to make sure of that,' Ravi said, trying to reassure the caretaker.

Subba Rao described in detail the whole visit including the arrangements that had been made by him and the food he had served.

'Did you serve paan or alcohol at any time?'

'No sir, my master was a teetotaller so there was no question of serving alcohol, and I did not serve any paan.'

'Tell me what happened this morning.'

'As usual I went with a cup of coffee at 5 a.m. but since there was no response to my knocking, I went back again at 5.30 and then at 6 a.m. When I knocked on the door at 6 a.m. there was still no response, but after the third attempt I pushed the door and it opened. On entering I discovered my master's body near the bathroom. Sahib had vomited in the bathroom and also in the bedroom. He looked unconscious so I ran to chhote sahib's room and knocked loudly. I was shaking from head to toe and could barely talk, but managed to convey the seriousness of the situation to him. Chhote sahib then rushed to his father's room, examined him and finding no sign of life, rang up their personal doctor and then his sister. The doctor reached in an hour's time, officially declared him dead, and then they shifted the body home.' Tears started flowing down his face as he relived the events of that morning.

Ravi let him settle down a bit and then asked casually, 'Was your master's window closed or open when you found the body, and was the air conditioner on?'

'It is September, sahib, and you know how hot and humid Delhi is in the rainy season, so the AC was on in the bedrooms at night. In fact, I closed the windows of both the bedrooms in the evening to prevent the mosquitoes from coming in. I also switched on the ACs when the sahibs were having dinner, so that the bedrooms would be cool when they go in.'

'Did you hear anything unusual last night?' Ravi asked.

'No sir, I had an undisturbed night and woke up only in the morning.'

This was quite possible, thought Ravi, considering the distance of his room from the family bedrooms. It had also been raining hard that night which would have further muffled any noises coming from Rao's room, he deduced.

At the same time as Ravi was speaking to the caretaker, Rahul was in the room of the security guard, Balram Singh, talking to him. 'Tell me about yourself and everything you know about your sahibs's visit.'

'Sir, I'm an ex-serviceman and got this job after retiring from the army. I do not know much about what went on inside the house as I am mostly at the gate,' he pleaded.

'Could an outsider have entered without your knowledge last night?'

'No sir!'

'Did you leave the gate unguarded at any time?'

The guard looked a little uncomfortable. He confessed that he had left the gate unguarded once that night. 'I had gone to get something for my masters from a nearby shop and delivered it to them.'

'What was it?' Rahul asked in a deeply suspicious voice.

The guard was quiet for a while.

'What did you go to get?' Rahul asked firmly.

'Paan . . . a . . . and a few other things.'

'What type of paan was it and what other things?'

'Sweet paan for the big sahib and saada, plain, for the chhote sahib, and some cigarette packets that chhote sahib had asked me to get,' he replied.

'Was this usual, or you brought it only on this visit?'

'Just this time sir. I thought I would do it as a special gesture on this visit as they had been very kind to me.

'Who told you chhote sahib ate saada paan and bade sahib ate sweet paan?'

'Chhote sahib told me about their preferences sir.'

'Hmm . . .' Rahul rubbed his chin thoughtfully. 'Did you hand over the paans to the caretaker or directly to the sahibs?'

'I delivered all this directly to chhote sahib's room sir.'

'After you got the paans, did you deliver them immediately or did you wait till the dinner was over?'

'I delivered them after dinner.'

'How were the sweet and saada paans identified?' The security guard had turned wary by now and the answers were coming slowly and after much deliberation.

'Sahib, the sweet ones had some grated coconut on top and were kept together with two lavangs, and the saada ones did not have any coconut toppings and were pinned up with only one clove.'

'Did someone give you any substance to put in the paan meant for your bade sahib?'

The security guard looked startled before answering 'no sir'.

'Since you left the gate unguarded, could someone have entered from outside?' Rahul asked.

'No sir, I had locked the gate before going,' he answered.

'Okay, that will be all.'

Ravi decided to leave and report their findings to the CP. They would decide the course of action after meeting the police commissioner.

Commissioner Bedi was disturbed by their revelations but happy at how much they had unearthed in a day, 'Well done, Ravi! I'm glad we decided to investigate his death. Let's take this case forward and quickly confirm whether the death was unnatural.'

Ravi promptly added, 'Sir, I suggest we conduct a post-mortem to rule out death by poisoning.'

'Go ahead, but do it as quietly as possible, since I do not want to tell the media anything until we have more proof. Get on with your work now, and let me talk to the home minister.'

Ravi returned to his office after the briefing to where Rahul was waiting for him.

'Chief, I don't know about you but I'm ravenous. Let's have lunch—there's rajma and paranthas in my tiffin.'

'Sounds good Rahul, let's eat,' Ravi responded enthusiastically.

That evening Ravi recalled that he had met Dilip Singh on a flight and he might be able to throw some light on his father-in-law's death. He dialled Dilip's number, 'Hi. Is this Dilip Singh? I'm DCP Ravi Sharma, do you remember me? We met on the flight from Bombay to Delhi.'

'Of course I do and what a coincidence!' he sounded drawn but eager. 'You know I was thinking of calling you up but did not get time to.' Then he was quiet. 'You must've heard about my father-in law's death . . . I've been busy receiving all the VIPs, including the Prime Minister, because my mother-in-law is in the US. She has asked us not to cremate him till she comes. We're therefore shifting the body to a mortuary. I am there now and have completed all the formalities. Can we meet in half an hour? I think there is much to discuss.'

Ravi was more than eager, 'That would be great! Will you come to the police headquarters?'

'Can we meet somewhere else? I do not want to attract attention,' Dilip asked.

'Ah yes, of course. I will be heading home in a while. You can join me there. It is near the headquarters. Please take down the address . . .' Ravi narrated the address and gave directions.

'It'll take me about forty minutes to reach there. Is that okay?'
'Oh perfectly! See you there.'

Meanwhile Ravi asked the intelligence department to send him what they had on Dilip too. On receiving the intelligence report, he headed home.

Once at home and waiting for Dilip to arrive, he went through it. He learnt that Dilip Singh came from an ordinary middle-class family and till his teenage years had an unremarkable track record. But once he picked up a cricket bat, the whole world knew his destiny. In his cricketing years, Dilip was a rare combination of steadiness and flamboyance and had been one of the best all-rounders in the world. Very soon in his career he had become the captain of first the one-dayers and then the test team. Ravi read that Dilip now owned a chain of hotels and malls that carried his logo—DS. He had recently retired from active cricket. He was married to Anu, Rao's elder daughter. He had become a partner in his father-in-law's company, and two years back, had added another feather to his cap by becoming a member of the Indian cricket board.

Ravi read the report carefully. He was impressed with Dilip's meteoric rise due to his talent in cricket. He thought that once a person attains fame, recognitions and laurels keep coming to him—fame attracts more fame!

Three

It was a landmark day in India's cricketing history. It was the day of the opening ceremony of the T20 League of India (TLI). The mood at the Ferozshah Kotla stadium in New Delhi was nothing short of carnivalesque. The music was loud and being played by a live band of youngsters who were a rage among the college youth. In the centre of the stadium cheerleaders dressed as celestial nymphs were gyrating to a spirited crowd. A shirtless hunk and a top 'item girl' from Bollywood, the Hindi film industry, were leading the show on the dais. The atmosphere was electric.

A huge crowd had been allowed in free to witness the historic occasion to give the series a boost. The country had never seen anything like this before. Besides the live crowd, the whole nation was glued to their television sets, eagerly watching the tamasha unfold.

Twenty20 cricket was finally set to begin with a bang. Or was it?

A few months back, the first-ever auction of players had been held at the Taj hotel in Mumbai. There were to be eight franchisees who were to bid for the Indian and foreign players and there was a professional auctioneer conducting the event. He was to be the sole arbiter in case of any dispute. Each franchisee had already received the rules for the auction and the composition of the players available for bidding. The TLI auction was not being broadcast live, but edited highlights had been released periodically by Ex-el TV, which had the sole broadcasting rights.

There was to be a 'base rate' set for each player, from which figure the bidding would begin. And all franchisees had a common upper limit or 'purse' above which they could not spend. Bids once placed could not be withdrawn. If due to any reason, some players were not bid for and the teams remained incomplete, there would be a second round of bidding. Everything had been planned perfectly, but things did not go entirely as planned . . .

Many players wanted to join TLI but the official cricket board had managed to dissuade several senior players from joining in. As a result, only second- and third-rung players were available for the auction. The bidding itself had therefore not been as enthusiastic as was expected. The franchise owners went through the motions and Ex-el TV tried to portray the event as an exciting and evolutionary one for its audience. But somehow the proceedings lacked zest. Nevertheless, the auction was completed and the teams were formed. And now the day of the opening ceremony had arrived.

Though cricket purists were horrified, to many youngsters in the country, Twenty20 cricket was thrilling, pulse-racing stuff that was about to catch the nation's imagination. They had gathered in huge numbers to witness this event. To them test cricket was like watching a stretched-out version of one-day cricket, and they had tired of it.

A youngster working for a BPO said, 'Who wants to spend five days following a game that seems to run in slow motion? It "tests" my patience.' There was a roar of appreciative laughter from his friends at the intended pun.

'There's no other game in the world that goes on for so long!' said another, who was a software professional.

'It must have been conceptualized by retired fuddy-duddies,' said an aspiring model, 'and it is watched by older fuddy-duddies, who have nothing to do but hang around a television, watching twenty-two "gentlemen" dressed in spotless white clothes and pottering about for days on end.'

'I think Twenty20 cricket is exciting, and I'll regularly come to the ground and watch the matches live every time they are held,' said another teenybopper.

There were three people who had visualized and planned the whole thing:

Surya Seth, a recently retired Indian captain;

Ramesh Patel, the owner of Ex-el TV; and

Sunil Mane, who was a former treasurer of the cricket board.

Surya surveyed the festive air with satisfaction. 'Ramesh, you've done an excellent job. You really know how to catch the pulse of the people, but where are the senior players from the Mumbai Maestro team?'

'I've only planned today's event. It's you and Sunil who have conceived and made the blueprint for the TLI—the name sounds good doesn't it? And about the players, I too was wondering why they have not turned up as yet. Well, the cars have started arriving, let's get this show rolling! We'll worry about the missing players later,' replied an animated Ramesh.

As soon as the franchise owners and players from all over the world started walking the red carpet, the music and dance went wild till it reached a crescendo.

Vikram Dutt the well-known commentator, who was to emcee the function, took the microphone, 'Welcome ladies and gentlemen, to a landmark day in India's sporting history. We are gathered here to flag off the TLI or T20 League of

India. I am sorry to inform you that some of our senior cricketers have been held-up in a traffic jam, but hopefully they will soon join us. I am sure all of us are looking forward to a delightful evening, where we will be treated to a world-class cultural extravaganza followed by the inauguration.' There was a huge uproar from the crowd.

True to his word, the hour-long cultural event was every bit a success, with the crowd enthusiastically participating in and applauding each performance. There was a show-match as well, after which Vikram Dutt took the microphone again, 'Friends, we are ready for the inauguration now, but first, a few words from Mr Ramesh Patel, the head of Ex-el TV, the main sponsor of the league, Mr Sunil Mane who has been a treasurer in the cricket board, and finally the man we all love, Surya Seth! Ladies and gentlemen, please give a huge round of applause to the three men behind the TLI!'

Amidst great cheer the three men stood on the dais. Patel being a man of few words lived up to his reputation. But Mane, for whom this was the platform from where he was going to launch his comeback to cricket administration, made the most of it. After having been cleverly ousted from his position as treasurer in the board, he had lain low for three years, but now he wanted to be back in action and somehow fulfil his ambition of becoming the board president. His speech was long and full of energy. He concluded with, 'Ladies and gentlemen, this is the platform from which I want to re-launch my involvement with cricket; let us together make this venture a big success. Now I'll hand over the mike to Surya Seth who we all love very much.'

As Surya took the microphone, there was deafening applause. His popularity had not waned a bit even though he had retired from active cricket more than a year back. He was a down-to-earth man and his speech reflected that.

'Thank you friends, it's great to be amongst all of you. As you know I love the game passionately and my idea of starting the TLI is to give back to cricket a little bit of what it has given me. We hope to make a lot of money out of TLI. And more money will mean better infrastructure and better prospects for Indian cricket. I can also assure you that we will do our best to make TLI as competitive and as entertaining as possible.'

Their speeches were followed by the official inauguration that ended with a brilliant fireworks display and the release of thousands of balloons with 'TLI' printed on them. While the crowd watched in delighted amazement, Surya took Sunil Mane aside and informed him that the five senior cricketers from the Mumbai Maestros for reasons unknown, had not yet left their hotel rooms.

Sunil Mane was furious, 'Let us hold an inquiry, and if there are no justifiable reasons we have no option but to suspend them from the tournament.'

The show had been a hit, but the organizers were anxious about how the league matches would go. Their anxiety sprang from the fact that there had been many hitches from the time of the auction itself.

If the inaugural show had hiccups, worse was to follow, as the organizers were denied the use of official grounds. They had to hire private ones and get them ready at short notice. They did their best, but the much-touted league matches fizzled out like a damp squib. This is what happened—

Mumbai Maestros were to play their first match against Hyderabad Diwans. But their top five players were suspended as they had failed to attend the official inauguration without giving any convincing reason. An inquiry had later revealed that they were in their hotel rooms but had not come out. The match was thus played with a weak Mumbai team.

It was a totally one-sided affair and the Hyderabad Diwans won easily, but the home crowd (the match was held in Mumbai) was restless and booed the organizers throughout the match. The ill-prepared grounds also worked against the teams, making bowling erratic and batting and fielding dangerous. This set the tone for the rest of the tournament at different venues, with the crowds slowly thinning out. With the initial enthusiasm dying down, TLI was jinxed all the way through with new problems surfacing at each venue. So by the time it ended, almost everybody had lost interest.

The three organizers knew who was behind it all but were powerless. The media declaring it the fiasco of the year did not help either.

Four

The cricket board was humming with more energy after the flop of the TLI. Sometime in the middle of the year another meeting was held to further diminish the euphoria of this first commercial venture in cricket. People in the cricket board had discovered that there was money to be made and self-interests to be looked at. Rajeev Kabra, a member of the cricket board, and the man he called 'boss', got together in the board office.

'Rajeev, the time has come to start our own league, now that Surya has shown us the tremendous potential Twenty20 cricket has. We will aim at something similar. We will call our league "ITL"—short for Indian Twenty League.'

'Yes boss, and by derailing *their* league we've also wiped out all competition. I think our own will do very well,' Rajeev simpered in agreement. He was a yes-man to his 'boss' and knew that any disagreement would not be taken lightly.

'Start working on the blueprint along with Manik Jindal and next week, we'll put up your presentation in front of the board. We need to also send feelers to good players around the world and start contacting sponsors.' He waited for the feeling to sink in because he knew Rajeev would take time to absorb the details and also what was to come next.

'And another thing: I think we should ensure that Manik is elected the chairman and is the official face of ITL. I want you to remain behind the scenes and take care of all the macro and micro level planning of not only ITL but our other ventures as well.'

Rajeev's face fell for a fraction of a second. To say that he was highly disappointed was putting it lightly, since he had taken it for granted that *he* would be the chairman of ITL whenever it was launched. But somehow he hid his feelings and agreed to the suggestion, even adding one of his own. 'And boss,' he said, 'we'll take the precaution of announcing the dates of the auction only when we have everything lined up, not before that. We don't want them to do to us what we did to them!'

The 'boss' gave a huge appreciative guffaw at this. They both knew they would pull it off. Rajeev joined in but noticed that he had never seen him laugh this much! Somewhere inside his brain he could see his 'boss' becoming larger than life. He had a sense of his intolerant nature which could destroy anything or anyone coming in his path. Rajeev's dread had made him used to obeying his mentor blindly, and within a week he had the blueprint for the ITL ready with Manik Jindal's help.

A special meeting of the board was called in Mumbai, and since the proposed agenda was of such great interest, almost all the state heads and administrative staff were in attendance. The president took the mike and called the meeting to order, 'Friends, as you all know, there's a single-point agenda for today's meeting—whether we, the official board, should start our own league matches or not. Although the TLI league has failed due to unknown reasons (there were knowing sniggers around the table, though nobody dared to say anything out loud), I feel the concept and idea are good and we as the official board can and should try to carry this forward. As you may be aware, the board has been doing very well since I have taken over, and we have been making a lot of money (there was a lot of table-thumping and hear! hear!).

'I wish to inform you that a blueprint has already been prepared by our team. We have all the details worked out including potential sponsors who are ready to pump in huge sums of money (there was more table-thumping and cheering). Now Manik will read out the plan to you in brief. Each of you will get a detailed copy later. After the presentation, there will be thirty minutes allotted for discussions before it is put to vote. Let me now hand over the mike to Manik.'

Manik, who had worked hard with Rajeev Kabra in putting together an extensive and comprehensive presentation, walked up to the podium amidst the silent and expectant air. He was a man of average height and appearance, but his education abroad had ensured that he carried himself well. He was crisp, lucid and informative.

'Dear friends,' he began, 'The Indian cricket board is by far one of the richest sporting bodies in the world. By launching ITL, which is our aim now, we hope to make further profits and expand our interests. We draw inspiration from something which has existed in the West for years. For instance, there are three American sporting bodies: the National football league (NFL), the baseball league (NLB) and the basketball league (NBA). They are the richest sporting leagues in the world, followed by the English football league (EPL). We are going to pattern our league on the lines of the NBA and the EPL.

'But before we jump to replicating that, let me give you some statistics that have to do with these two leagues and will be of interest to us. The NBA was established in 1949 and it has twenty-two league teams. This year, its profit was

10.6 million dollars for the earnings of 3.8 billion dollars. The English Premier League football comprises twenty clubs. It is a corporation where the twenty clubs are shareholders. Their earnings have increased from 750 million euros in 1996-97 to 2,273 million euros in 2006-07!' He paused and waited for those present to assimilate what he had said. He knew they would be curious after this.

'For both, the earnings come from television, internet and mobile telephony and also merchandising, sponsorships and ground-signage rights.' He could see several heads nod in appreciation. It all seemed simple enough.

'Our aim should be to become *the* richest sporting body in the world. And we can easily reach a figure of 2 billion dollars next year if we launch the ITL. That would translate to an eight-fold increase in revenue since 2005!' There was a loud gasp and some murmurings, but everyone soon fell silent and he continued, 'In fact the ITL is going to be huge, and if we handle things well, in another three years we can catch up with the EPL and the NBA and then target American football. Our earnings can only increase exponentially, since our biggest asset is our huge population, whose spending and purchasing power is going up. I visualize sponsors falling all over themselves to reach out to this billion-strong number of cricket crazy fans. I envisage that it will only be a matter of time before we become the richest sporting body in the world!'

Everyone was fascinated and interested. There was money to be made!

Manik continued, 'Now about the ITL—it will comprise eight teams, eight franchise owners and sixteen players in each team to begin with and the matches will be played over one and a half months. We have worked out the logistical details which will be circulated among all of you. We will make this work. Let me end by saying that the future looks very bright and rosy for Indian cricket and for the board!' He smiled and almost took a bow. This time there was resounding applause. As he took his place, a few members next to him even patted his shoulder appreciatively.

However, a lot of the applause was also self-congratulatory, since the members were enthused by the huge financial projections that were made. Especially the unstated prospect of the slice of golden pie that would be theirs to spend as they liked, with hardly any questions being asked!

There was a round of general discussion, then the president took the mike again and spoke, 'We now have to elect the chairman of our league. Any suggestions?'

The 'boss' spoke first, 'I propose the name of Manik Jindal.'

As if on cue, Rajeev Kabra stood up, 'And I second it!'

The members were so euphoric that they were not in a mood to oppose anything, and Jindal was elected chairman of the newly formed ITL unanimously. Manik Jindal was himself beyond ecstatic. He later called a press conference to announce the date of the auction.

After this it was smooth sailing, as the auction took place and the teams were formed. It was a tremendous show, and the dates for the first tournament were announced. As expected, sponsors jostled with each other to fill the coffers of the board and its fortunes skyrocketed.

The ITL was modelled on the same lines as the sporting bodies in the West. There were eight teams, four from the metro cities of Mumbai, Delhi, Chennai and Kolkata and four from smaller towns—Mohali (Punjab), Rajasthan, Hyderabad and Bengaluru. There were a minimum of sixteen players in each team from which the player's eleven were chosen, but some richer teams had broader bench strengths.

There was a sense of déjà vu in the nation when the event actually began. However, this time round since the jamboree was being organized by the official board and the sponsors were the who's who in the industry and from Bollywood, the response was huge with Manik Jindal as the chairman and the master of ceremonies. A huge stage had been erected on a cricket ground and the event was being officially started.

Chairman Jindal took the mike, 'Ladies and gentlemen, welcome to the launch of the official cricket league of India, the ITL or the Indian Twenty League!' No one could miss the stress on the word 'official' and a buzz went round the packed stadium.

'The Indian cricket board has always done its best to try and make the country the topmost cricket-playing nation in the world. And we are all gathered here to launch the ITL, which is the next step in that direction. Let me announce proudly that we have been able to attract the best talent not only from within the country but from all over the world. Our sponsors too are top-notch as you will shortly see. You will be entertained with a stage show, the likes of which you would have never seen. And after the cultural event, there will be a fireworks and laser display. So, ladies and gentlemen, fasten your seat belts and enjoy a great evening!' The air crackled with excitement amidst the thunderous applause. Manik smiled in self-appreciation. It was all working! *His* plan, *his* ideas.

The inaugural event and the tournament itself held from 15 September to 30 October was professionally organized and the viewership was unprecedented. The ITL, as opposed to the TLI, had started off well.

Far removed from all this, Sunil Mane, the cricket board treasurer was awaiting the arrival of a few special guests in his bungalow in Delhi, which he used whenever he visited the city. This visit had been planned well in advance. The special invitees he was waiting for were Ramesh Patel of Ex-el TV and Surya Seth, one of India's most iconic players who had recently retired from professional cricket. They were disappointed with the way their league had been demolished by the bigger, brighter ITL.

When they arrived, Mane said to Patel, 'Ramesh, you said you had a plan, tell us about it.'

Ramesh answered, 'I've told my team of ace reporters to keep their eyes and ears open to find out any activity that can be deemed suspicious. My men are all veterans at this and very soon I expect to have enough ammunition to shoot down our opponents and pay them back in their own coin! Ajay Shukla is especially good. I'm confident he will soon bring in results.'

'Right then, let's enjoy ourselves this evening and plan on how to revive our league. What do you think Surya?'

'I'll go with Ramesh!'

'Agreed then, Ramesh we depend on you! When we've gathered sufficient dirt, we'll throw it hard at them, and sure enough it will stick to tar their image. We'll plan our strategy as soon as we get some masala from your reporters.'

After the other two had left, Mane asked his housekeeper Vijay to get him his usual Bloody Mary. Vijay knew how to make the perfect one—a big glass of Bloody Mary with just the right quantity of vodka and fresh tomato juice, the rim liberally salted, and a couple of slices of lemon stuck to the mixing stick. He took it to his employer's bedroom. He also kept a bottle of Worcestershire sauce that his master liked to add just before he started drinking. Mane was in the bathroom, so Vijay quietly put the drink and the sauce bottle on the table and left. It was 11 p.m.

Emerging from the bathroom, Mane, as was his habit, added some sauce, stirred it in and propping himself on the bed, started sipping his drink. He switched on the TV. The Bloody Mary was good, just the way he liked it, and when it went down his throat there was a pleasant and familiar sensation. He felt warm and good. He especially loved the tangy taste of the lemon and salt. Life had been good to him. He knew it would get better.

He continued sipping and watching his favourite reality show as he reflected on the events of the evening. The meeting had gone off well and he knew he could trust Ramesh Patel to quickly come up with enough dirt to nail the people who had tried to ruin his life.

He was feeling comfortably drowsy now. He remembered he had to call his wife but he had consumed too much alcohol and it was hitting him. He decided he would sleep it off and call her in the morning.

A little while later, he felt restless and nauseous. Before he could get to the bathroom, he vomited all over the bed. He ran to the bathroom to clean up, where he vomited again. Somehow he got back to the bed, pulled off the covers and threw them into the bathroom. Mane decided he would sleep directly on the mattress. He lay down again, but there was a strange and unfamiliar weakness. Should not have had so many drinks, he chided himself.

He had another bout of vomiting followed by severe loose motions. After it had happened the fourth time, he was scared. It was 2 a.m. now. He wanted to call Dr Sobti whom he had consulted when he was in Delhi before, but he could not find his cellphone to make the call. There was no landline in this house, as it was not needed. I must go to

Vijay's room and ask him to fetch the doctor, he thought, and dragged himself to the door although he was feeling extremely weak. But however hard he tried, the door wouldn't open! He tried to shout but his voice was feeble—it came out in an inaudible croak.

His mind remained clear though his body seemed lifeless. Is this a heart attack or food poisoning? he thought to himself. He wondered if someone had locked his door from outside and taken away his cellphone.

He would never know because he suddenly had convulsive fits and became totally paralysed. It was three in the morning and it had been a night of struggle. But it was over at last and finally he found everlasting peace.

In the morning Vijay Kumar found his master's body and called Dr Sobti, who certified that the death had been due to a massive heart attack. They managed to inform some local relatives. The body of Sunil Mane was flown to his hometown the next day for cremation. There was good coverage of his life history on all the channels. Leading newspapers of the country also carried his obituary since he had done a lot for Indian cricket during his tenure as the board treasurer.

Five

At the police headquarters the death of a senior member of the cricket board had caused quite a stir. It was not uncommon to see the press hanging around at all times of the day for any piece of news or evidence the police might unearth or give a statement about.

So when Rahul announced, 'Chief, a reporter from Ex-el TV is waiting to see you,' as soon as Ravi entered the crime branch headquarters the next day, Ravi wasn't surprised.

'Okay, call him in. Let's see what he has to say,' he said walking into his office. His office reflected his personality—sparsely furnished with very little on display. There was a rare photo of a smiling Gandhiji on the wall facing his table, which was uncluttered with only a PC, a notepad and a pen stand on it. The upholstery on all the chairs was an understated cream colour. The room was absolutely tidy and had a certain elegance to it.

Sitting across his table was a young and bespectacled reporter in his mid-thirties. He appeared casually dressed and laid back but his crisp manner as he introduced himself revealed that this was a man who knew his job. Coming straight to the point he said, 'Hello, I am Ajay Shukla from Ex-el TV. I am here to discuss two murder cases that may prove of interest to you. At present these are with other police stations, but the officers there have not yet realized how significant these cases really are.'

Ravi sat up straight. He wanted to hear what this man had to say. 'Okay, what's their significance?' he asked. 'And also, what's *your* interest in them?'

Ajay spoke with ease, 'At present our channel only wants to request you to take over these cases and conduct preliminary investigations. I promise you that you will not regret it and will come to know about their significance as you proceed with your investigations.'

'Which cases are these?'

'The Rupali and Sunanda murder cases. I suspect they may be connected in some way to the S.N. Rao case that your branch is investigating, though as of now I cannot state precisely how. I'll send you the details if you wish.'

Ravi was intrigued. The suggestion of a senior reporter of a major TV channel that they look into two cases had to have *some* importance. He thought for some time and then nodded, 'We will look into these as per your suggestion. But there better be something to it.'

Ajay Shukla looked satisfied. 'Like I said, you will not regret it,' he repeated, shaking hands before departing.

Ravi immediately turned to Rahul, 'Can you look into these two cases? I think I will concentrate on the Rao case and you can handle the ones Ajay Shukla was talking about. We will update each other regularly.'

Rahul nodded. If there was a relation between the three cases, he wanted to know. Two days later, he entered Ravi's office with the requisite files. 'Chief, the case files were in poor shape and badly worded. I've taken out excerpts and followed them up with the cases in detail.'

'You did not have any problems acquiring them?' Ravi asked.

Rahul laughed, 'No, the inspectors in charge of the police stations were more than happy to reduce their workload by getting rid of a case each!'

Ravi smiled resignedly. He did not know who to blame, the police force which was overburdened with work or the system which promoted passing-the-buck. He took the files from Rahul.

CASE EXCERPT 1
Death in a Medical College campus
20 August 2007

On the morning of 20th of August 2007, when many of the staff members in the medical college campus were out on their morning walk, there was a commotion near the C-type flats. Someone had got burnt and a crowd had gathered there. People came to know that it was Rupali Agarwal, the wife of a Dr Agarwal. Somebody had tried to smother the flames with a blanket and she had been rushed to the ICU. She never came out of her coma and died within two days.

CASE EXCERPT 2
Death in a South Delhi bungalow
30 August 2007

Neela had as usual returned home and turned on the lights in the porch and those in the drawing room. The switched-off lights gave her an ominous feeling that something was wrong. After taking off her outdoor footwear, she hurriedly wore her indoor rubber slippers and rushed towards the stairs to climb up and see what Sunanda, her sister's nurse, and Shweta, her sister, were doing. But when she went near the stairs, she got the shock of her life. She found Sunanda lying there with her neck at a grotesque angle, and very still.

For a few moments Neela was paralysed with shock and could not move, but slowly she forced herself to go near. She got down on her knees and looked for Sunanda's pulse but could not feel it ...

Ravi smiled at the drama in the writing, 'Rahul, I can see a closet writer in you. I do not know of any other policeman who would volunteer to write out a case again!'

Rahul seemed pleased, 'You never know chief, I might compile them all into a book after I retire. And I've already thought of the hero's name—DCP Ravi!'

'Thank you Rahul. That is a compliment, but tell me about the cases in detail now,' Ravi smiled.

'First let me tell you about the death of the nurse in the South Delhi bungalow,' Rahul responded, and began to read from the sheets in his hand:

'Yuvraj Singh, a wealthy real estate dealer, turned to social work in a big way as he got older. He became a well-known figure in the city and was on backslapping terms with the who's who in Delhi including the top brass from all political parties. His wife Yashodhara had been famous for her bonsais and paintings and had held several exhibitions. They had two daughters, Shweta and Neela.

'When Shweta was twenty-two and Neela twenty, their mother developed breast cancer of a particularly virulent type and passed away. For Yuvraj Singh, her loss was difficult to bear. His health slowly deteriorated after that and five years later, he had a heart attack and expired. The girls were then respectively twenty-seven and twenty-five years old.'

'Who was the person that died?' Ravi interrupted.

'The nurse. She comes in later. Now, Neela had a formal degree in software and soon got a job. It wasn't that they needed the money; their father had left enough cash, property and stocks for them to lead a very comfortable life. The house itself is huge and worth several crores. But Neela, like her father, is a workaholic. She not only goes to work but also prefers driving herself instead of being chauffeured around. Mr Mehra, their financial advisor and family friend, is their only pillar of strength.

'Shweta the elder daughter was badly affected by her parents' death. She became quiet and withdrawn, and any attempt to force her into something she did not want resulted in her throwing tantrums and turning almost violent. She wanted to be left alone on the top floor, all the rooms of which she slowly occupied, filling them up with her artwork and the many bonsai plants that she had inherited from her mother. These she carefully nurtured and added quite a few of her own.'

'What about the staff?'

'When the parents were alive, the Singhs had a staff of two drivers, a cook, a housekeeper, two servants and a gardener working for them. After their death, Neela retained their gardener, one driver, cook and the housekeeper. Things seemed to be settling down a little after their parents' death, when Neela started feeling that Shweta was becoming more and more withdrawn and increasingly difficult to manage. Finally she realized that she could not ignore the issue any longer.

'She therefore consulted Dr Sanjay Nanda, a psychiatrist. Dr Sanjay came home, saw Shweta and diagnosed her with schizophrenia. By the way, chief, this is a condition where a person gets dissociated from the real world. The doctor told Neela he would start the treatment and also provide her with a nurse-cum-caretaker that he felt Shweta would soon need. He was as good as his word and in a week's time he sent Sunanda to meet Neela.'

Ravi looked up, 'Sunanda was the nurse who died?'

'Yes chief.'

'Okay, read on.'

'Sunanda was so young, charming and competent that within a week, Neela had no hesitation in requesting her to move in full-time. Meanwhile, Neela's interaction with Dr Sanjay increased because of Shweta and slowly a friendship developed. Dr Sanjay is good-looking with a pleasing personality. He was around thirty years old when he first met the Singhs and had been practising for about three years since his MD. His parents are in Bangalore with his elder brother who works for a software company and he was living alone in Delhi. Within six months of their meeting, Neela and Sanjay decided to get married. And considering that "Yashodhan", the Singhs' house, was so huge, he moved in with them. Sanjay and Neela occupied the ground floor rooms where Neela's parents used to stay when they were alive.'

'So, when the nurse died, Neela, Sanjay and Shweta were the full-time occupants. What about the staff?'

'All of them left by two in the afternoon.'

'Anyone else who was close to the family?'

'Yes, their financial manager, Mr Mehra.'

Rahul could see his senior was pensive. He waited for some time and then continued, 'For a year things were quiet and peaceful in Yashodhan. Neela and Sanjay were busy with their work and with each other. Sunanda was equally busy with her work as caretaker of both the house and of Shweta. Shweta had improved a lot under Sunanda's care. She had again started spending many hours quietly working her magic on her bonsais, till there were fruits on her orange and lemon trees, the loveliest flowers on the bougainvilleas. Her pride was a banyan tree with a number of hanging roots. The trees were neatly arranged all over her big room that received plenty of light through a huge window that looked out to the back of the house.

'A year and a half after they got married, Neela and Sanjay decided to take their first holiday together since Shweta was in the capable hands of Sunanda. But when the couple returned home, things were not the same. Shweta had become withdrawn and peevish once again, and even Sunanda's serene face looked strained and unhappy.

'She told them she was finding it hard to manage Shweta who was refusing to listen to her. With great difficulty she was able to make her eat a little and take her medicines. Sanjay increased the dosage of her medication and started giving it to her personally.'

Ravi said, 'The background and psychology of the people in the case has been brought out quite well Rahul. But I think we need to read up on schizophrenia because a complete understanding of Shweta's mind is very important. Go on now!'

'Chief, I've become particular about the psychological aspect after you told me how it helps in solving cases. To continue, Neela tried to cheer Shweta up and spent as much time as she could with her, but somehow she had become Shweta's biggest enemy and her sister would not allow her to come near her. Under Sanjay's intensive care, Shweta improved again and even went out a couple of times with Sunanda. Neela was particularly upset that Shweta was openly hostile towards her and Sanjay had to start giving his wife sleeping pills to help her sleep at night.

'Another six months passed in this tumultuous fashion and then the tragedy occurred. The following account has mostly been obtained from Neela: On 30 August 2007, Neela as usual returned home at 6.30 p.m. The house has a remote-controlled security gate that can be opened without getting down from the car, and the house itself is surrounded by high walls so no one can enter uninvited. Neela came in through the gate and it closed behind her as she drove in. She then parked the car and let herself into the house with her key. She, Sunanda and Sanjay all had their own remotes for the gate and also keys for the main door, so that they could come and go whenever they liked without disturbing the other two. Normally, the lights outside the house and in the corridor would be turned on but that day they were off. Neela felt uneasy at this but reasoned that probably Sunanda had forgotten to switch them on.

'She entered the house and turned on the lights of the porch and drawing room. After taking off her sandals, as I had mentioned earlier, she found Sunanda lying there, with her neck twisted in a bizarre fashion and her body very still. Fearing the worst she immediately called Sanjay and asked him to rush home with an ambulance. She did not say that Sunanda was dead but that she had suffered an accident.

'Meanwhile, she ran up the stairs to check whether her sister was okay. Shweta was carefully watering her bonsais and seemed completely oblivious to what had happened downstairs. Neela did not disturb her and tiptoed back down and waited for Sanjay to arrive.

'It took half an hour for the ambulance to reach the house. Sanjay was shocked and extremely disturbed when he saw Sunanda. After examining her, he helped the attendants in strapping her and then shifted her on to a stretcher without moving her neck. They tried artificial respiration in the ambulance itself as they rushed her to the hospital. But everyone knew that Sunanda was no more. In the meantime Neela went upstairs again to check on Shweta and to give her something to eat. Her sister was now walking up and down and looked highly agitated. Had she seen or heard anything? Neela thought as she tried talking to her. But finding her unresponsive, she kept Shweta's dinner on a table and asked her to have it. She then quietly sat in the room for some time before going down again. She could sense that her sister was heading for a relapse—'

'Were the police called in immediately?' Ravi asked.

'No chief, they were informed much later.'

'Hm, well, go on.'

'Sanjay came home very late from the hospital and in an unusually dishevelled state. He had known Sunanda for long and seemed badly affected by her death. He said that the body had been kept in the morgue and would be cremated the next day after Sunanda's parents arrived from Ghaziabad. Neela told him about Shweta and with visible difficulty, he forced himself to go up and take a look at her. He came down after a while and said he had given her a strong sedative with milk and that she had gone off to sleep. He would review her medicines in the morning.

'The next day Sunanda's parents came and insisted on a post-mortem. The post-mortem concluded that Sunanda's death was caused by her spinal cord being severed when she fell down the stairs. The fall itself was probably an accident. But her parents were not satisfied with the "accident" theory and lodged a police complaint.'

'Rahul, investigate Sunanda's case in more detail. Go to their house and meet the people there. We will discuss the second case, Rupali's, a little bit later.' Ravi found his mind wandering in several directions and decided to sit calmly for a while to collect his thoughts.

'Yes chief,' Rahul responded after some time. He knew that the case was in good hands, and since Ajay Shukla had asked them to look into it, they were sure to find a link to S.N. Rao murder case. Things were getting complicated but experience had taught them that before situations get solved, especially those related to murder and crime, they reach a stage of confusion.

Six

When Rahul rang up Yashodhan, the residence of the Singh sisters the next day, Neela picked up the phone. Her voice was soft and distant. Rahul introduced himself and said he would like to meet all the family members and staff the next day at 9 a.m. Neela said she would make sure everyone was present.

Yashodhan was a neat, compact bungalow in grey sandstone, well-covered from the roadside by a perennial climber. Rahul was impressed with the sense of order the house seemed to exude.

Neela and Sanjay received Rahul and he noted that behind his carefully groomed appearance, Sanjay looked strained. He told them he wanted to take their statements and preferably one by one. Sanjay immediately got up and said he would leave and return when Neela was done.

When they were seated, Rahul began, 'Madam, the police may have already met you, but our branch has recently taken over this case and I would like to ask you a few questions.'

'Please go ahead,' replied Neela quietly. She was tall and dusky and was dressed in a pastel silk sari. She wore very little make-up and had the understated elegance of the very rich. She could not be called beautiful, yet had an attractive face and an arresting personality. Ravi had taught Rahul to observe the gaze and the body language of people he was questioning and Neela's eyes were wide open and honest. She also appeared calm and collected.

'Can you tell us everything you know about Sunanda and her death?' Rahul asked.

A wave of pain passed over Neela's face as she spoke, 'After our parents passed away, my sister became very quiet and reclusive. She would stay alone for hours together and avoid company. That is how I met my husband Dr Sanjay Nanda, as I needed a good psychiatrist for her. One of my colleagues had suggested his name. Sanjay diagnosed her with schizophrenia and agreed to treat her. He did a very good job too as Shweta improved tremendously under his care. We became close to each other, since Sanjay visited frequently. Soon we decided to get married. Meanwhile, Sanjay suggested Sunanda's name as an expert caretaker-cum-nurse for Shweta and so Sunanda came to stay with us.'

Rahul was watching her keenly to detect any false note in her narration, but she continued to speak calmly and in an even tone. He was also relieved to see that she looked him straight in the eyes while talking.

'Sunanda was a very nice girl and so very competent! After she moved in, I did not have to worry about my sister. She and Shweta got along well and were very friendly with each other. After almost a year of our marriage, Sanjay and I decided to take a holiday, and when we returned, my sister's condition had taken a turn for the worse. She again became irritable and difficult. The only person she now listened to was Sanjay. Poor man, he had to spend a lot of time with her after he returned from the clinic to keep her in good spirits. He had to also increase the potency of her medication.

'During this time she had developed a severe antipathy towards me that I found difficult to bear. But Sanjay told me it was usual for a schizophrenic to develop animosity towards the very person they were closest to and I had to console myself with that.

'Coming to the day Sunanda died—it was like any other. I returned from work and opened the remote-operated security gate and drove in to find the house in total darkness. I quickly parked the car and came inside after opening the door with my key. On entering, I switched on all the lights and—'

'Wait a minute madam, what was the time, and where were the gardener and the driver?'

'I did not look at my watch but I must have left office as usual at 6 p.m. and I normally reach home by 6.30 p.m., so it must have been around that time. The gardener had gone home between two-two-thirty after finishing his work and the driver must have been sent off by Sunanda. I used to leave him home so that he could help Sunanda with any outside work. You see, Sunanda had taken up the dual responsibility of nurse-cum-housekeeper that also involved a lot of outside work. We have a cook and servant coming in the morning but they also leave around 2 p.m. Sanjay and I both drive our own cars.'

Rahul nodded, 'Please go on.' He could sense a slight dread in her voice as if she was scared of recalling that incident again.

'After switching on all the lights, I went towards the staircase to go up and see what Sunanda and Shweta were doing, and I found Sunanda lying near the stairs, her neck twisted. I could not feel her pulse or see any other sign of life, so I quickly phoned Sanjay to reach home with an ambulance as fast as possible, saying Sunanda had suffered an accident. Sanjay was here in half an hour and Sunanda was shifted to a hospital. But we came to know she had died long back. While waiting for Sanjay, I checked on Shweta and found her working unperturbed with her bonsais. To my mind, Sunanda's death should have been an accident, since I cannot imagine her being killed by anyone.'

Rahul said, 'Thank you madam, you have been very lucid and informative. Please come to the police station at your convenience to sign your statement.'

Neela nodded and left the room saying she would send Sanjay in.

As Sanjay walked in, Rahul thought that the doctor probably belonged to the new breed of doctors who always looked well-groomed and stylish. He also seemed prone to self-promotion as was evident by the number of his photos that hung around the drawing room, showing him receiving awards from various dignitaries. Ravi wondered how a doctor who had to work with psychiatric patients could always present such an unruffled look. Their police psychiatrist permanently had a harried and crushed look to him. Even today Sanjay was perfectly turned out, without a hair or crease out of place, in a pink linen shirt teamed with white trousers.

As he slowly lowered himself on the couch, Rahul asked him, 'Could you please tell me what you know about Sunanda and her death?'

The pain in Sanjay's eyes was evident as he began to speak. 'I have known Sunanda for the past many years. She came to work for me when she was a young girl of twenty-two. I trained her in handling psychiatric patients and she was a fast learner. Since she did not have a proper place to stay, I got her an assignment to take care of an old patient of mine suffering from Alzheimer's disease. When that patient passed away, I sent her here to take care of Shweta. She was really very good at her work and diligent by nature. I feel responsible for her death since I brought her here, but I'm sure her death was a natural one due to a fall down the stairs.'

His eyes misted a little and he paused, unable to go on for some time. Then collecting himself he continued, 'It was Neela who rang me up to tell me about Sunanda's accident, but when I reached home she was very much dead.' His shoulders sagged as he sighed and stopped again.

Rahul watched him carefully as he began once more, 'She was her parents' only child, and they must have suffered a terrible shock. That is why they want to rule out any unnatural cause of death. But I must try and convince them to withdraw the police complaint so that we can all be at peace again. Nothing is going to emerge from this inquiry. That is all I have to say.'

It was Rahul's turn to speak now. 'Since we've started the investigations, we cannot withdraw the case now. Hopefully you are right and we will reach the same conclusion. But one last question, do you play cricket or do you know anyone from the cricket board?'

Sanjay looked up, confusion visible in his eyes. 'I do not understand the significance of your query but to answer your question—yes I do play cricket at an amateur level but do not have any connection with the cricket board.'

'Thank you Dr Nanda for being so cooperative. I would like to meet the staff now. And please come to the police station at your convenience to sign the statement you have made.' Rahul stood up and shook hands with Sanjay. He watched him as he walked away slowly, his shoulders still drooping in sadness.

Rahul then questioned Uma, the cook, who told him, 'I liked Sunanda, except for one habit of hers—she used to get many calls on her cellphone and leave the house for a couple of hours, and tell us not to inform Neela beti about this. On the day of her death, I had left by 2 p.m. as usual and do not know what happened after that.' Rahul made a note of this.

The Premier Murder League

Then it was Kamini the housekeeper, then the gardener and the driver. Rahul knew that even though they stay outside the house, gardeners and drivers generally know a lot about the families they work for. He knew that an informal chat with them could reveal a lot of relevant information.

Rahul casually asked the gardener if either Sanjay or Neela had come to the house in the afternoon, the day Sunanda had died. The answer was prompt, 'Neela memsahib had not come, but doctor sahib had come home at 1 p.m. and left by 2 p.m., a little while before I myself left the house.'

Rahul was disappointed because the information did not help him. Sunanda's time of death had been fixed between 4 and 4.30 p.m. Had Sanjay come again after the gardener had left or did Neela come early, commit the murder, go back and return later to 'discover' the body? Rahul wondered. He would have to make enquiries at Neela's office and find out if she had left during the daytime.

'Did the cook and housekeeper leave before, or after you?' he asked the gardener, who seemed to be waiting for his questions.

'Both of them left at 2 p.m. together and I left only around 2.30 p.m.'

Atmaram the driver had been working with the family for the past ten years. 'Sir, she was a very nice lady and all of us liked her,' he said, referring to Sunanda. 'Doctor sahib had come home at 1 p.m. that day but left around 2 p.m. just before I left. Nurse madam came to see him off at the door, and that was the last time I saw her. In fact she told me then that I could leave for the day as there was no work for me.'

'Tell me a little about your duties.'

'Neela memsahib and doctor sahib drive their own cars. I have to only maintain their cars for them and take the cook, housekeeper, or Sunanda madam anywhere they want; and if the work was done by 2 p.m., as it usually was, Sunanda madam used to send me home. Since they have given me a cellphone, they could call me in the evening again if they required me.'

'Tell me anything more you know about Sunanda madam.'

Atmaram spoke slowly as if thinking aloud, 'Nurse madam used to go out almost daily. Usually she would be alone, and occasionally she would take Shweta memsahib with her. When on her own, she would ask me to park the car and go off on a walk. Sometimes she would be gone for as long as two hours. When she would bring Shweta memsahib along with her, they would go to a mall or a big public garden and walk around. They would spend an hour or two there and I would wait for them in the parking lot.'

Rahul jotted all this down. He then went back inside the house and took leave of Neela and Sanjay. From there he drove to their financial adviser, Mehra's office. Mehra owned a chartered accountancy firm called 'Mehra and Mehra' that took care of the family's finances. After his brother had passed away, he and his nephew were running the firm.

Currently in his seventies, Mehra was dressed in an old-fashioned, grey buttoned half-jacket over his starched white shirt and a grey bow tie. The office too was completely old-world with huge upholstered sofas and armchairs, teakwood cupboards and bookshelves with camouflaged lighting. Mehra came forward to meet him and shook hands. After seating him on one of the huge sofas, he himself sat down on his equally huge armchair behind his desk, bridged his fingers and asked, 'What can I do for you?'

Rahul smiled. 'Mr Mehra, we are investigating the death of the nurse at the Singh residence and would like you to tell us all that you know about them.'

Mehra spoke slowly, 'Shweta and Neela are like my daughters and I feel responsible for them especially after their parents' death. But after Neela's wedding to Sanjay, I distanced myself a bit. I confess that I do not get along so well with him. After the nurse's death, I called up Neela and commiserated with her. I also told her that I would always be there for her whenever she needed me. But about the actual death, unfortunately, I do not know anything.'

'Sir, can I ask you why you do not get along with Dr Nanda?' Rahul said.

'I feel he is overly inquisitive about the state of his wife's finances,' saying this, Mehra did not seem to want to speak any further.

Rahul felt this was an important point. 'Thank you sir for your help. I'll get back to you again if needed.' Mehra nodded. Rahul was amused to see that his fingers remained bridged throughout the conversation.

~

In his review session with Ravi, Rahul spoke his mind, 'It could be any one of the three, since Shweta was at home when Sunanda fell and both Sanjay and Neela had keys to the house; they could have entered quietly, committed the murder and exited. Shweta seemed unaware of anything untoward having happened, so the first suspect has to be Neela, second Sanjay and third Shweta. The driver and gardener could also have done it on one of these people's behest, since they seem very loyal and didn't appear to particularly like Sunanda. We should not rule that out. Then there is the old housekeeper Kamini who sounded resentful about Sunanda, but I doubt she is a suspect as she was open about her dislike for her. The house itself is very secure, so it has to be an insider's job.

'Also, the driver has volunteered the information that Sunanda used to often disappear for as long as two hours. Was she meeting someone outside the house? I need to work on all these angles and try to find an answer.' Rahul looked up at Ravi when he finished.

'And why has Ajay Shukla asked us to look into this case? It had to be of some significance. Was it in any way connected to the Rao murder? Hopefully we will soon find out,' Ravi added. He concluded by asking Rahul to make discreet enquiries at Sanjay's clinic and to set up a meeting with Sunanda's parents. He also told him to confiscate all their cellphones and send them for transcription. He asked him to go to Sunanda's bank and also meet Shweta at Yashodhan. There was definitely something wrong in this case.

Seven

After arranging for his father-in-law's body to be kept in the morgue, Dilip headed straight to Ravi's house. It was not difficult for him to reach there as Ravi's instructions had been quite clear.

Ravi lived in a residential complex in a society allotted to the police due to its proximity to the police headquarters. The flats were a pleasant combination of sandy brown and brick red and had an unpainted and natural look to them. They blended well with the surrounding greenery. Dilip drove in and parked his car.

He rang the bell. 'Hello and welcome. We were waiting for you,' Ravi said. Then he turned to introduce his junior, 'This is ACP Rahul Singh.' Rahul and Dilip shook hands.

It was a three-bedroom flat with a spacious terrace. Even though the construction seemed old it had a cozy air to it.

'Why did you want to meet me?' Ravi asked, guiding Dilip to a couch in the living room.

'I wanted to sort out some misgivings that I have in my mind,' Dilip answered, sinking into the sofa. He was relieved that there were no constables to listen to their conversation. 'My father-in-law was a good man whom I respected a lot. He did have quite a few medical problems, but the way he died suddenly has perturbed me especially since it happened away from home, where help could not reach him on time.

'Another thing that bothers me is that Vineet, his elder son was with him at that time and they were not on the best of terms. Maybe I'm being morbidly suspicious, but something tells me that all is not well. I've always trusted my hunch up till now and my uneasiness also springs from the fact that my father-in-law had been acquiring powerful enemies who did not like his values. For quite some time now, I've been getting negative vibes from some people he knew and interacted with and had the foreboding that something terrible might happen. That's why his sudden death makes me anxious.'

'Who are these powerful enemies?' Ravi asked.

'Some members of the cricket board. I cannot give you any definite names till I am certain about their involvement. And there's something else I want to tell you. About seven months back, Twenty20 cricket was introduced in India. You must know about Surya Seth's Twenty20 sponsored league, TLI?'

'Yes I do know that it was launched with much fanfare, but has almost evaporated without a trace due to some controversy,' Ravi said, his eyes narrowing in concentration.

'Right. I'll tell you the inside story. The aim of the league was to get a mixture of foreign and Indian players and some talented youngsters who had not yet played for the nation, build up teams and have them play sponsored games against each other. The idea was to unearth fresh talent in the country and also to make money. Sponsors were found and the auction for the players was held. But most of the star players who were contracted with the official board were not allowed to join TLI. Also, the TLI was denied use of the official grounds and had to prepare second-rate venues in a hurry. The final nail in the coffin was that some major players from the Mumbai team did not turn up for the inaugural ceremony, although they were in their rooms in the appointed hotel! Later they were disqualified from playing the rest of the league as a disciplinary measure. But all these little things kept adding up and there were very few spectators for the matches. The sponsors lost a lot of money and the tournament was a total washout,' Dilip said.

'Do you have any idea who all were involved in this? It can't be the work of one person,' Ravi said.

'I do not know who was actually involved. My father-in-law and I were not consulted and it is difficult to take names.'

'Are you implying that the TLI fiasco is in some way connected to your father-in-law's death?'

'I think so,' Dilip answered as he shifted on the couch, 'Let me tell you why. Mr Mane, the former treasurer of the board and one of the people behind TLI and my father-in-law were good friends. When Mane was dishonoured and removed from the board my father-in-law was upset and had voiced his displeasure at the manner in which this was carried out.

'Then when Mane tried to resurface along with Surya Seth to launch the TLI league, it was sabotaged. My father-in-law again voiced his displeasure, but his concerns were brushed aside.

'Mane died a broken man. For a few days after Mane's passing away, my father-in-law seemed to be brooding a lot. He felt the extreme methods that had been employed against Mane had resulted in stress that had probably led to his death. He also felt that the board was acquiring a negative image which could have long-term repercussions.

'Finally, he decided to speak out—this time at the next official board meeting. A condolence message was passed at this meeting and the general verdict was that it was unfortunate that Mane had died, but the board could not be held responsible in any way.'

Ravi and Rahul were listening intently as Dilip continued, 'My father-in-law was dissatisfied with the response of the members, but he had to remain silent or quit the board. I could see that he was in a dilemma about this. Then, about a month back, two things happened: I got an anonymous call to stay away from my father-in-law. And he himself told me something potentially explosive. He had come to know that huge kickbacks were being received by the current treasurer of the board and some others close to him for TV rights and ground advertisements. And a substantial portion of this money was being siphoned off to fund a major political party. They were probably paying all parties, but the principal amount seemed to be going to the party that the important members of the board were affiliated to. He said he was still deciding what to do with this information and told me not to reveal it to anyone for the time being.

'I have been very uneasy and deeply disturbed since then. And when I came to know of my father-in-law's sudden death, I somehow felt that I had almost expected this to happen. I am nearly certain his death was not natural. It could be his son Vineet or his enemies in the board. The only thing I do not know is whether there was any other reason to do away with him. I keep asking myself, would they murder one of their own members, that too such a senior one, just because he might stand in the way of their nefarious financial activities? Or did they suspect that he knew too much and could prove dangerous to them?

'I have been confused, and did not know what to do, till I remembered being acquainted with you on a flight and decided to come and consult you. But before that, you called yourself, why is that?'

Ravi then went on to tell him that the home minister had called the commissioner of police and how the latter had told them to visit S.N. Rao's farmhouse. He also described what they had found and Dilip was horrified.

'I strongly feel that a post-mortem should be performed,' he responded.

'Your mother-in-law is in the US, right?'

'Yes, she arrives back tomorrow night.'

'After she comes, persuade her to agree to a post-mortem before the body is cremated. I can arrange for it so that only the three of us, the hospital dean and the doctor who'll conduct it will be in the know. This doctor is a forensic expert and a personal friend. After performing the post-mortem, the body can be cremated, and we'll see how to proceed further.'

'Yes, let's do that.'

Dilip sat for some time thinking deeply. He then thanked Ravi and Rahul and went home feeling disturbed and hoping he had not been seen by anybody.

After Dilip left, Ravi turned to Rahul, 'Bring me whatever information you can gather about Ramesh Patel, the owner of Ex-el TV. If Dilip thinks the TLI fiasco had something to do with S.N. Rao's death, we need to know more about the men behind TLI. Mane has died, and we know almost everything about Surya Seth, the third man behind TLI, since he is so famous. However, we know very little about Ramesh Patel who was its main sponsor.'

'Sure chief, I'll see what I can get on him by tomorrow,' Rahul said.

By next day afternoon an intelligence report on Ramesh Patel, the owner of Ex-el TV, was on Ravi's desk:

Ramesh Patel was the son of a rich diamond merchant from Gujarat. After completing his MBA from Harvard, he had worked in the field of media management in the

US before heading back to India. He was only thirty years old when he started Ex-el TV along with a partner from Hong Kong.

Ex-el TV was the first private channel to be started in India and it took off with a bang. It also coincided with the introduction of colour TV in India and proved so successful that Ramesh Patel soon became a very rich man. He bought off his partner and there was no looking back after that. He is said to be a very astute businessman with friends and supporters in all political parties. Recently his foray into cricket in the form of a sponsor of TLI has proved to be a failure. It has probably been the only major setback in his career.

On the personal front, Ramesh Patel is married to Neeru, whose father is also a diamond merchant. Theirs is a highly successful arranged marriage that has been running smoothly. They have two sons, one of whom is a director in Ex-el TV, and the other has taken up the traditional family business of diamond merchandising.

By the time Ravi finished reading, Rahul came into his office. Ravi said to him, 'Failure of TLI must have hurt a high-profile businessman like him badly. I wonder how far he will go to avenge it.' It was a thought that bothered Rahul too.

Eight

Ravi reached the hospital at 5 a.m. the next morning, where Dr Madhukar Gupta was already waiting for him. S.N. Rao's family had agreed to the post-mortem. The doctor was in his late forties and one of the best forensic experts in the country. Tall and lanky, he had thick, black hair and wore square-rimmed glasses. Almost always dressed in full-length white overalls, he was so passionate about his work that very few people even knew he had a wife and family. He was also a brilliant speaker and had a great sense of humour. Ravi respected him immensely since he had helped him in solving many cases. In the last couple of years, both had become good friends.

The post-mortem room was big and stark, with white walls and a very strong smell of formalin. Ravi had attended enough post-mortems with Gupta to have become used to the smell but the formalin still bothered him. He quickly accepted the mask and zero-power wrap-around glasses offered by his friend to reduce the smarting it caused his eyes. They shook hands and exchanged pleasantries but said little beyond that. Both of them knew it was important to concentrate on the task at hand.

The naked body of Rao was placed on a steel table lighted up brightly by an overhead lamp, and beside him was a tray on wheels that had the instruments Gupta would need during the post-mortem.

The procedure was quickly completed within an hour, and Gupta gave a running commentary even as he performed it.

'As you can see, I'm first opening up his abdomen and will collect some samples. A surgeon's job is tough considering his subject is alive, but *my* job is easier. I don't have to worry about bleeding or other complications so I can work very fast. My surgical instruments are also less refined.'

Ravi listened attentively as Madhukar continued, 'I'm going to take samples of urine from the urinary bladder, stomach contents and bile from the gall bladder. I will also cut out some congested parts from his kidneys where blood had collected. These samples will be packed and sealed in labelled formalin containing jars that I have kept ready, the formalin acting as a preservative, as you are aware. Ravi, please hand the jars to me as I call out which ones I need.'

They finished with the abdomen and Gupta sewed it up again.

'Now I cut open the chest, which is slightly tougher, and have a look at the heart and lungs. As you can see, both look congested. We'll preserve parts of them too.'

Ravi handed over two more labelled jars for the heart and lung samples.

'Now, we do some carpentering. Hand me that drill, Ravi.'

'I've seen you do this so many times but it never fails to amaze me that you use a regular carpenter's drill to open up a human skull!' exclaimed Ravi.

'Yes, but it also has a small saw attachment that makes it a little different. The human skull is very tough as it has to protect the most fascinating part of the human body. I've now cut open a slice of the bone and kept it aside. Next, I remove the covers and here it is, our most important organ—the brain! Let me see, there are patches of congestion here too. Let's preserve them. Ravi, hand me that jar labelled "brain". Now I simply put the slice of bone back and it stays in place. Okay, we're done. Let me clean him up a little and cover him up again neatly with this new sheet. No one will know that we've performed a post-mortem unless they remove the wrap.'

'That was very fast Madhukar. Now what will you do with all these samples after labelling and sealing them?'

'Ravi, for now I'll put them in that first cupboard from the left and keep them locked there. If you'll do that for me, I'll finish cleaning him up. Later, I'll have the samples sent to the forensic lab.'

When he was finished, Gupta explained, 'As you have seen, there is congestion of all the major organs that indicates a poison of some kind was used that caused oxygen deprivation. I cannot reach a conclusion till we get a forensic report. But I can tell you this much that I did not find evidence of a heart attack, brain haemorrhage or any other natural cause leading to sudden death. Let's wheel him back to the mortuary.'

As they were leaving the mortuary after replacing the body, Gupta thought he saw a figure disappearing rapidly down the corridor. *Had he imagined it?* He concluded that he had and did not mention it to Ravi.

After the post-mortem, Ravi decided that he needed to go back to the farmhouse once again and conduct some more investigations. He was worried now after what his friend Madhukar Gupta had told him. If the death was not natural, there had to be more clues around the scene of death that would give him pointers. Hassan drove him there and he tackled the two employees once again.

Ravi spoke to the caretaker Subba Rao whose room did not reveal much. He seemed to be a religious person with many pictures of gods and goddesses on the walls. There was also a photo of his family who were at Hyderabad. He said he had left them behind for the schooling of his children. There was a small television in the room, a bed, a cupboard and a folding chair made of iron. Ravi's conversation with him did not bring out anything significant either.

He next spoke to the security guard in his room.

Balram Singh's room was well-equipped, with a television and a music system too. There was a small sofa and a steel almirah with a lock. Ravi made him open the lock and saw some liquor bottles and clothes inside. But there was an inner compartment that was difficult to see and it was also locked. Ravi insisted on it being opened. The guard pretended to look for the keys and behaved as if he could not find them.

Ravi threatened the guard with his revolver, 'If you don't find it soon I'll have it to break it open!'

Balram Singh looked extremely disturbed and flustered. 'Sorry sir, I've found it,' he said, as he opened the inner compartment. Ravi peered inside taking the precaution of making the guard stand in his line of vision, but he could not see anything. However, on putting his hand inside he could feel bundles of paper. When he drew them out, he found that there were five new bundles of notes each with '10K' written on them with a pen.

'Where have these come from?' he asked pointedly.

The guard wiped sweat from his face and said, 'Sir, I save most of my salary here since I want to buy a house. My family lives on my pension so I do not have to send any money to them.'

Ravi made a mental note that it would be a good idea for someone to visit the guard's house because he knew Balram Singh was lying. The notes were new, sealed and looked uniformly alike and the serial numbers were in sequence.

The money had to have come at one go since they were all crisp new notes. It was definitely not gradually accumulated salary money.

'How much were you getting paid here?'

'Sir, I have been getting five thousand rupees a month plus free boarding and lodging.'

'I'll have to confiscate this now and if all is well, I will return it to you later,' he spoke curtly to the guard and stuffed the money in his evidence bag.

While Ravi was questioning the two employees, he had asked his driver, constable Hassan to go over the grounds surrounding the house to look for any empty containers. Ravi now saw that Hassan was waiting for him with a plastic bag in his hand from which he brought out four containers.

'Sir, I found this squarish small box near the window of that bedroom.'

Ravi saw he was pointing to the bedroom that had been occupied by Vineet, Rao's son.

Hassan continued excitedly, 'The second one I found in the corner of the lawn.'

It was a small bottle similar to the dispensing bottles used by old-time doctors. Ravi smiled inwardly. So some doctors still used them!

'This third one, a small bottle with a dropper, I found under the bougainvillea bush, and the fourth, a container also with a dropper, I found in the gutter outside the gate. It was hidden in the tall grass that is growing in and out of the deep gutter.' Hassan took Ravi to the spots where he had found them.

'The first three are fine, but I am curious to know how you found the fourth one; it must've been buried deep and hidden inside the thick grass,' asked Ravi.

Hassan grinned and took out a contraption from the haversack on his back. It had two foldable aluminium rods joined together at the bottom to a small steel tray with strong magnets stuck at the base. 'This can be plunged in to pick up solids hidden in grass or mud and it also attracts metallic objects. The height of the rods is adjustable because it has hinges, and you can also swing it around to break the grass on top to reveal what lies below. Most objects have some amount of iron in them, and the magnets help in picking them up from deep and inaccessible areas. Even those that do not have iron can be brought up because of the heavy tray,' he explained proudly.

'Where did you get this from?' Ravi asked, astonished.

'Sir, I designed it myself, I am not too educated, but like to design utility items like this. It is a handy implement since it folds up completely and occupies only the space of a quarter-plate.'

'It is ingenious,' Ravi said appreciatively. 'We should supply one to all the police chowkis and perhaps apply for a patent. You might become very rich!'

'Thank you sir; when you have the time I'd like to take you home and show you my workshop where I've designed many more things.' Hassan seemed duly pleased.

Ravi patted him on the back, 'I'll certainly come Hassan, well done!'

They returned to the house and labelled the containers with information of date, time and location, and then sealed them. There were two experiments yet to be conducted.

Ravi explained, 'I am going to lock myself inside Rao's bedroom and scream on the top of my voice. I want you to go to Vineet's bedroom and see whether you can hear me.'

Ravi did this and the constable rushed back, 'Sir, I heard your scream!'

'Ok, now go back again. This time I will close the windows and switch on the AC. You also do the same, and tell me if you hear anything.'

This time the constable had heard it again but the sound was muffled. In all probability, in deep sleep, Vineet must have missed it. And in any case, Rao could not have shouted loudly because of his weakened state. It was also raining heavily that night and this would have further dulled any sound coming from his room, Ravi reasoned.

Should I arrest the guard immediately on suspicion, or keep him under surveillance? Ravi wondered. He decided to arrest him. They had enough grounds for doing so. He had bought the paans on his own initiative and delivered them. He looked guilty and money that seemed to be from a dubious source had been found in his almirah.

'Hassan, formally arrest this man on suspicion of being involved in S.N. Rao's murder and make a note of the confiscated money. We'll have to try and trace the source. I'll meet the commissioner and report to him.' Hassan was only too happy to follow his senior's instructions. After all, he had played an important part in the investigation!

They then drove back to the headquarters with the handcuffed guard. Away from all this, preparations were on for the minister's cremation. His son Vineet and son-in-law Dilip had arrived at the hospital and carried the body home in an ambulance. There was a big crowd of VIPs outside who wished to see off the body. Some of them were close friends and relatives accompanying the minister's body to the crematorium. The women stayed behind.

Significantly, no one from the cricket board attended the ceremony.

Nine

The next day early morning, Ravi got a call from Dilip. 'Have you heard? All the TV channels except ours are broadcasting that my father-in-law's death was probably a murder. How did they get wind of this?'

Ravi was concerned, 'It must've been the post-mortem. We can trust Dr Gupta completely, but someone must have noticed that a post-mortem was being conducted on Dr Rao's body and leaked it to the press. But it does not matter, it had to come out someday. I was only hoping that we could have made some more progress before the news broke out. Let's take this positively. Since it's out in the open, we might get some fresh leads. Also, don't worry, we're on the job of finding the killer and will get to the bottom of it.'

Ravi was right. He received another call from Ajay Shukla, the reporter who had asked him to look into the South Delhi and medical college murders. He wanted to share some information and to come and see him. Ravi told him to come over immediately. He could never have guessed how important this meeting would turn out to be.

The reporter was there within an hour, his tall frame looming in Ravi's office.

He shook hands with Ravi, 'Good to see you again!'

Ravi nodded and indicated the chair across the table.

Ajay continued, 'I have sensitive information that may or may not prove useful to you in this case but I have a feeling it will . . .'

Ravi could see the hesitation in his speech. To encourage him to speak he said, 'Every bit of information is important to us. Please go ahead.'

'The incident I'm talking about occurred a month before the minister's death. The owner of our channel, Mr Ramesh Patel knows about it since I had kept him in the know and we've been keeping the information under wraps since then. But when the news of Rao's suspected murder hit the channels, Mr Patel advised me to meet you with a proposal. If the information we provide proves useful in unravelling the case, you must promise that we will be the first ones to receive any breaking news. Especially if it has to do with the cricket board. After all, there is a huge incentive in it for us to get even with the concerned for sabotaging our league. You know about that I presume?'

Ravi had been listening carefully. He smiled, 'Yes, I do know about it and I promise we shall give you any breaking news we get.'

Ajay gave a relieved smile. He must have been under pressure from his channel head for this news. 'Thank you. A month back I went to the Kay-Pee mall to shop. Just as I was going to enter the mall, I saw Rajeev Kabra of the cricket board exchanging something with another man. Mr Patel had told us to keep our ears and eyes open to detect any suspicious activities of the cricket board. So as soon as I saw Kabra carrying out this secretive activity, I was immediately on alert.'

'Hmm,' Ravi was thinking, 'Do you remember the date and time of this meeting?'

'Yes, the date is easy to remember since it was 16 August, and the time was 4 p.m.—I usually have a coffee at that hour.'

'Excellent! Please continue.'

'I couldn't see what was exchanged, but both men put their hands in their pockets as if to hold on to what they had given each other. It must have been something small, since I could not make out what it was. After the exchange they started walking away from each other. Since I knew who Rajeev Kabra was, I was able to recognize him in spite of the huge dark glasses and hat he wore. In fact I could have recognized him in any kind of disguise. I have been studying him so closely! But I am digressing. I decided to follow the other man to find out his identity. This man was short, fat and balding. He got into his Zen and I followed him on my bike. I was lucky since he drove a short distance and then stopped in front of a commercial building.'

'Okay. Do you remember the name of the building?' Ravi asked.

'No, but I know the place well and can give you directions.'

'That's fine then, go on.'

'I waited across the road to see where he would go. He parked his car in front of an office that said "Ace Detective Agency", opened the lock of the agency door and went in. I was intrigued. What was Kabra doing with a private detective and why this hush-hush exchange in front of a mall? I reasoned that the detective had handed over some material, probably in a storage device—a CD or something. I am assuming it was an investigative report on someone. And Kabra in return would have given him the payment. This had to be something small again because I could not see it. Could it be gold or diamonds in a small pouch because it certainly wasn't a wad of notes.'

Ravi was intrigued. He said, 'It could be. Please continue.'

'I called up my boss from my cellphone right there. I felt it might be significant enough to inform the owner of our channel. Mr Patel heard me out but decided that we would not do anything immediately. Then I got absorbed in another lead story and forgot about this incident. But when I heard that a senior member of the cricket board had died, and later that it may have been a murder, somehow my intuition told me that the meeting between Rajeev Kabra and the detective may in some way be linked to the death. In any case, by then we had decided to follow up any lead, however remote.'

'Good thinking, and was there a link?'

'I'm coming to that. After I was through with my lead story, I decided to pay a visit to the Ace Detective Agency. The name "Ranjit Arora" was prominently displayed on a table stand. He was the owner of the agency and was luckily in his office when I reached there. He was the same short, balding man I'd seen that day. I decided that the best approach would be to come directly to the point. "Mr Arora," I began, "I am a reporter with the Ex-el channel. And I am aware of your interactions with the cricket board, especially your meeting with Mr Rajeev Kabra. I saw both of you exchange something and put it in your pockets on 16 August at 4 p.m. in front of Kay-Pee mall. My sixth sense tells me that the exchange may have had some connection to the minister S.N. Rao's death. Do you want to come clean, or would you like me to go to the police and let them question you? If you like I can negotiate a deal for you from our channel and also keep your identity hidden—if you will give us the information."

'Ranjit Arora maintained a poker face and said, "I don't know what you are talking about."

'"Well, if that's your stand, it's fine by me. But I strongly suspect that what happened that day has a link to Rao's death because Kabra is a member of the cricket board. And if you do not come clean, I *am* going to the police." That seemed to soften him up a bit and he was slightly more forthcoming. He said, "I did have a meeting with Rajeev Kabra but it is not connected to this incident. However, the information may be worth money, so let me think things over carefully before taking a decision. Meet me in a week's time."

'I thought I had my man. "No, I'll come tomorrow same time when either you will give me the information or I will approach the police," saying which, I got up and left.

'Now this Ranjit Arora, as expected, is a wily customer. He was just trying to fob me off to buy time. He would've told me to get lost but since I mentioned the word "police" he was restrained. I found out later that he had been working in another detective agency at a very junior level and had the guts to start his own from scratch. He must've worked extremely hard to reach this level.'

'He'd probably used every trick in the book to claw his way up,' said Ravi.

'And he certainly did not want to throw it all away,' Ajay answered. 'So, when I went back the next day, he assured me that the material exchanged had nothing to do with Rao. He showed me the file dated 14 August on his computer. It revealed that a search had been conducted on the new members of the board. I knew the man was lying, since the material looked too innocuous to be real and had possibly been created after our meeting. He'd probably deleted the original material and added the new one using the same date on the file. I had been checkmated and Arora knew that. I reported back to my boss and we decided that the best plan of action would be to come to you since you were handling the case.'

'You did the right thing. We can do with every kind of lead in this case,' Ravi said, falling back into his chair.

'I'm sure that the proprietor of Ace Detective Agency is lying, and the material that had changed hands was in all likelihood linked to Rao. You can approach the detective, conduct a shakedown and get the correct facts, but please remember your promise that our channel will be the first to receive any important news.'

'It's a deal. And if you get any other leads, keep us informed,' Ravi responded.

As soon as Shukla left, Ravi decided he would go and get the information out of the Ace detective guy, if it wasn't already too late.

Ravi followed the directions Ajay had given and reached the office of the agency within twenty minutes. It helped to have a police jeep. Luckily for him the agency was open, and that meant the proprietor was in. Ravi rang the bell and the 'ace detective' himself opened the door. Seeing the uniformed officer he turned pale. Shutting the door quickly so that no one could see them, he asked Ravi to sit down before going back to his own chair.

Ravi introduced himself, happy at the response he had generated. A flustered subject was more likely to come out with the truth! For a few minutes he let the tension build up as he casually looked around the office and then began, 'Mr Arora, I think you know why I've come. But to refresh your memory, you did a job for the cricket board in the month of August that is directly related to the death of the sports minister, S.N. Rao. I want you to tell me about it.'

The detective looked relieved then a little angry and cursed, 'I knew that saala reporter would fill you with lies! The work had nothing to do with S.N. Rao. I had told him that the file handed over to Rajeev Kabra on that day had to do with some investigative work I'd done on the new members of the board and I showed this to him too.'

Ravi smiled grimly, 'I know that was the story you tried to sell to him, but he wasn't convinced. You must know the extent of loss suffered by their channel when some members of the board sabotaged their league. He came to me today and told me of his suspicion that the real investigative report had to do with Rao and it was *your* report that led to his death.'

The detective continued to fib that he knew nothing of what Ravi was talking about and tried to placate him by saying he would give him any information he could gather in future relating to the case. But Ravi could sense that this man was hiding what he knew. 'Mr Arora, either you give me the correct file immediately, or I arrest and charge you on the suspicion of hiding sensitive information in a criminal case and abetting murder.'

Ranjit Arora thought for some time. He must've thought that an arrest at this stage of his career could prove extremely harmful, so he decided to come clean. 'I'll give you the correct information, but you must believe me when I say that I did not know why I'd been asked to conduct the investigation. You must also protect me from the board members who hired me, since they are powerful people and can ruin me completely.'

'If it is proved that you are not involved in the murder directly, I'll see that you're not harassed, but give me the correct information first.'

Feeling a little reassured, the detective took Ravi to his house, removed the pen drive from below the pile of papers in a cupboard drawer, and gave it to him. He had copied the file on to this storage device and then deleted it from his computer before Ajay Shukla's second visit. He had later felt he should not have preserved the material; but to him information and data were invaluable assets. One never knew when they could be traded for money!

This had worked in Ravi's favour.

'Mr Arora, this had better be the correct file, or you'll be in deep trouble. And just to be on the safer side, you'd better come with me till I've ascertained that it is the correct one. You have not committed any crime if you did not know the purpose for which you were commissioned to prepare a report on S.N. Rao, but if you cause obstruction in a criminal investigation, that will be a crime, and we won't spare you.'

Ravi drove at a manic speed to the police headquarters with the pen drive in his pocket and the chastened detective sitting beside him. He then plugged the device into his PC and went through the file.

There it was, the full details of S.N. Rao's life, with appointment schedules for the coming month, including the dates of the farmhouse visit with his son!

Ravi turned to the detective and spoke in a harsh tone, 'You can leave now, but keep your mouth shut. If even a whiff of this meeting reaches the board members, we'll arrest you and make sure your licence is cancelled!'

The scared detective promised not to speak a word and left hastily.

Rahul had just walked in and Ravi briefed him on the progress he had made.

'Chief, I hear that the media's going berserk. As soon as they got wind of the post-mortem, all channels have started speculating about the possibility of Rao's murder. The media frenzy is literally hitting the roof.'

'Rahul, we both know that television thrives on cases like these, when many hours of broadcasting time can be occupied endlessly giving the "breaking news", "covering new leads" and "interviewing experts". We should've expected this. As soon as they got a whiff of the word "murder", the excitement generated was bound to be tremendous. In fact I expect it to get worse. I was hoping to keep our investigation under wraps till we had gathered some more evidence, but things are now out in the open. And I think we will need to take some action. Rahul, let's first question Vineet as he was present at the time of his father's death.'

As Rahul walked beside his chief he had a smile on his face—they were making progress and this could be the mother of all cases he'd done so far!

Ten

Since Rahul was on his own in nurse Sunanda's suspected murder case, after interviewing the family of three he went to Sanjay's office the very next day. He had fixed up an appointment with the receptionist and had given his name as Sukhbir Singh.

Sanjay's office was in a posh locality in one of South Delhi's commercial areas. The building was spanking new with a tinted glass façade. It had high-end offices of lawyers, doctors and other professionals with a list at the lobby in brass lettering. There were four wings to the building, A, B, C and D, with four lifts for each wing. The six-storeyed structure had granite flooring and stairs that shone like glass. The elevators too were really chic, with a recorded voice announcing the floors. The whole building was barely short of being a five-star hotel.

Rahul whistled as he took in the high-class surroundings—it must have cost the builder a small fortune to build this, and even more to these professionals to be able to have an office here! Rahul had seen Sanjay's name in the lobby—

Dr Sanjay Nanda, MD
Consultant Psychiatrist—A/4/2

That was probably Wing A, the fourth floor and second office, he assumed. He thought about asking the receptionist, then decided against it. He almost ran up the four flights of stairs—he knew he needed the exercise.

Rahul was pleased that he had guessed right—office no. 2 had Sanjay's name on the door in highly polished brass letters. Just outside the office was a shoe rack where everyone entering had to place their footwear. Another shoe rack had rubber slippers in various sizes that one could wear. The reception area had three uniformed attendants with a logo on their shirt pockets that read A+ Securitas. Rahul knew that they were one of the most expensive agencies in the city.

Then he looked around and spotted the receptionist. There was a man in plain blue clothes standing right next to her. The third person he saw was a nurse who was going in and out of Sanjay's observation room. All three were neatly dressed and well turned out. There were two toilets, one with 'Doctor/Staff' and the other with 'Patients/Attendants' written on the door. Some office, he thought, wishing he could afford one as plush as this one. No chance, he mused, as long as he continued to work for the police department!

He walked over to the receptionist and said, 'Hi, my name is Sukhbir Singh and I have an appointment with Dr Nanda at eleven.' It was ten forty-five then.

The receptionist smiled and scrolled through the list on the computer screen. The she nodded and pointed to a seat.

Rahul waited about half an hour after which he explained to the receptionist that he had to rush off and would be back as his problem was not that serious. He smiled wryly to himself and decided that he had seen enough. The receptionist gave him another appointment. She looked like she couldn't care less. *Dr Nanda must have enough patients queuing up to see him.*

On his way out, Rahul started chatting with the lift attendant, 'I went to Dr Nanda's clinic, but when I found out his charges, I ran away. I had gone to get treatment for my sleeplessness, but I would have lost more sleep after emptying out my pockets to him!'

The attendant laughed, 'Each of these offices costs 1.5 crore rupees, minus the interiors, so they *have* to charge exorbitantly to recover that money. Dr Nanda, however, has a good reputation. He started here only a year back but is doing very well. His practice seems to be well-established.'

Rahul made a mental note. 'I think I'll come back if my sleeplessness gets out of hand. I'll also earn some more money so that I can pay his fees,' he said jocularly as he got off the lift. He could hear a chuckle behind him.

Back at his office, he wrote out the day's report to consolidate his thoughts. He wondered whether Sanjay had taken a loan from a bank. He put a junior on the job and then spent the rest of the day in routine work on other cases. Tomorrow he would go to meet Sunanda's parents.

~

The next day, Rahul left early morning and drove to Ghaziabad to visit the Pandeys. He had their address and phone number from Sunanda's post-mortem report and had called them up to inform them of his visit. Ghaziabad was a relatively quiet suburb of the city although it was expanding rapidly now, and Rahul could see huge building complexes sprouting like mushrooms. From what Rahul knew, Mr Pandey, Sunanda's father, had retired from the army as a havaldar. Sunanda was their only child.

Rahul found the house easily. It was part of a colony of small independent houses, but theirs was the best maintained. The garden was neat and rather green, and the house itself was in very good shape and looked freshly painted. There was a red Maruti Zen parked in the garage. Rahul pressed the bell and an elderly gentleman with a drawn face opened the door. Rahul politely introduced himself and said that he had come to meet them in connection with the case.

The elderly gentleman was Sunanda's father. His sad eyes directed him to enter the drawing room and sit on a sofa. As he entered, Rahul's eyes fell first on a big garlanded photograph of their daughter hung on the main wall of the drawing room. Sunanda's father went inside the house and Rahul took in the surroundings quickly—the small house was neat and well-decorated. With the way it looked, he assumed that Sunanda had been earning well enough to contribute to the upkeep and maintenance of the house.

Pandey came in with a glass of water, which Rahul graciously accepted and, taking a sip, sank back into the sofa. He asked the father, 'Mr Pandey, please tell me something about your daughter.'

A cloud of sadness appeared in the father's eyes and his voice came out almost in a whisper. Rahul noted that his hands were shaking a little, 'My daughter always wanted to be a nurse. So after completing her graduation she did a course in nursing. She passed with first-class marks and was slated to join a government hospital. However, we were keen on her joining a place with more income because I had bought the land for this house and had to repay the loan. So she joined the hospital where Dr Sanjay Nanda was working. They got along well and he understood our financial needs. After a few years, he got her a very lucrative residential assignment—that of taking care of a patient suffering from Alzheimer's disease. She was the mother of a member of the cricket board . . .'

'How long did she work there?' Rahul interrupted.

'About a year or so I think,' Pandey replied, looking down at his hands. It was as if he was reliving all the incidents in their lives. 'The lady died in a year's time but her son was generous and appreciative of Sunanda.'

'Did you know him?'

Pandey nodded.

'Who was he? Do you know his name sir?'

Pandey was slow to respond, 'Kabra . . . yes, it was Rajeev Kabra, I remember.'

Suddenly, as if on cue, an elderly woman entered with three mugs of tea. Her face was also downcast like the man's and Rahul assumed she was Sunanda's mother. She kept the tray on the table and sat heavily on a chair. The husband and wife began to talk in a low voice. However, Rahul's mind was working very fast. This was the first reference to a member of the cricket board! He seemed to be on the right track. There had to be a link between these two murders. Now he had to figure out how Sunanda's murder was connected to Rao's murder. *Was this the connection Ajay Shukla had wanted them to investigate?*

He turned to the father, 'Please tell me more.'

'After the old lady passed away, Sunanda again went back to work with Dr Sanjay Nanda, who had his own clinic by now. Then the present assignment came up—of caring for Shweta.'

'Tell me a little more about Sunanda,' Rahul asked.

He could see the eyes of both the parents well up with tears, but the father spoke, 'She was a good daughter—no less than a son. She knew how hard I had worked all these years but managed to save little so she took excellent care of us, sending ten thousand rupees a month regularly, so that we could be comfortable. She got this house built on the land I had purchased and even bought us a car. She came home twice a year and we visited her twice a year, when we were allowed to stay with her for the weekend. She was very happy and contented except for the last month or so when she did not seem her usual self. She was going to visit us the next month; and we wanted to persuade her to get married and settle down. But then she died . . .'

Mrs Pandey burst out crying, 'Sunanda was such a good girl. She troubled no one, hated no one, then why this cruel death? We have to know whether her death was an accident or a murder. It's not fair . . .'

∼

Driving back, Rahul's mind was full of questions and thoughts. The Pandeys seemed to be better off than they should have been on the pension of a retired havaldar and the income of a nurse. How was Sunanda able to send home ten thousand rupees every month? What was her salary? And how could she afford to build them a house and buy them a car?

He swerved his jeep towards Sanjay's clinic. The answer definitely lay somewhere there. Come to think of it, Sanjay had seemed unusually perturbed at Sunanda's death. He decided he had to go back to Sanjay's consultation chamber again. He made straight for the South Delhi office and this time he introduced himself to the lift attendant and said they had met the day before.

The attendant smiled, 'Earned some quick money to pay the doctor's fees?' *He had remembered!*

'No, I am not a patient. Actually I'm a private detective employed by Dr Sanjay Nanda's wife and I need some information.' Slipping a hundred rupee note into the attendant's hand he said he wanted some frank answers. The attendant looked amused; he knew all the gossip that was to be known in the building and was more than willing to share it with anyone. The money was a bonus!

His revelations filled Rahul with excitement, but trained as he was not to show any emotion, he kept his cool and prodded for as much as he could get.

The next day Rahul had the delicate task of speaking to Shweta. Neela opened the door when he reached Yashodhan. As Rahul entered he looked around and noted yet again that the house was spick and span, both from inside and outside. Neela too was her fastidiously groomed and elegant self. However, Rahul was amazed at the simplicity of her dress and demeanour. From what he could make out, she was a very rich woman but believed in work; she had servants but opened doors herself. Any other woman in her place would have become a social butterfly and enjoyed life. He had to respect her for that.

As they exchanged pleasantries and small talk, he noticed that she was not as composed and in control as when they had met previously. He knew that a death in the house could be unsettling but the strain on her face seemed to extend beyond that.

'You must be missing Sunanda now that she is no more,' he began cautiously.

'Of course, she was indispensable and also, frankly, was able to manage and relate to Shweta more than I could in recent times. My sister, ACP Singh, has been distancing herself from me and it hurts very badly.' Neela spoke in sad, measured tones. There were tears in her eyes that she was fighting hard not to shed.

Rahul did not quite know how to handle an emotional situation. 'Can I meet Shweta and ask her a few questions?' he asked almost brusquely in an attempt to hide his discomfort.

Neela collected herself a little. 'Yes, please go ahead, but be careful not to excite her in any way. Could I get you tea, or something cold?'

'No, a glass of water would be fine.'

Neela herself got the water and Rahul gladly drank from it. Then he casually asked, 'Don't the servants come in the evening at all?'

'No, we don't like servants to come in all the time, so the cook prepares dinner for the night, which we microwave and eat. I don't mind cleaning up. Earlier Sunanda used to help me. Poor thing, I wish she had not died! It is a big load on my mind. I've decided to give financial assistance to her parents so that they are taken care of but I'm sure no amount of money can compensate for the loss of a daughter.' Neela sighed deeply. She really seemed weighed down by sadness.

'That is indeed kind of you,' Rahul pitched in, glad to be able to have a normal conversation. 'Please don't worry, things will settle down. Most probably the death was an accident, but we have to be sure. Now if you don't mind I'll spend some time with your sister.' Neela showed him the way, but did not accompany him upstairs.

Rahul knocked on Shweta's door although it was open. The first thing he was struck by was her beauty. She had a baby-fresh, pink complexion, big, light brown eyes, long and thick hair, and although she was short and slightly plump, the overall effect was stunning. If he had not already known that she was schizophrenic, he would never have believed it.

'Good morning Shwetaji, I'm Rahul Singh. I am a friend of Sanjay's. I've heard a lot about your bonsais and have come to see them.'

Shweta hesitantly extended her hand to Rahul and briefly shook it.

She had the banyan bonsai in front of her and seemed to be working on it lovingly. Rahul went around admiring all the plants, especially the flowering bougainvilleas and poinsettias. There were also some lovely lemon, orange, custard apple and chikoo bonsais with plenty of fruit on them.

'How long has it taken you to grow these trees?' he asked, sweeping a glance at them.

Shweta smiled and said in a low, clipped tone, 'Ten years.'

'Wonderful! I just love them,' he exclaimed, even though he hated the concept of artificially stilting a plant's growth and including wiring to make it a dwarf tree.

'You should see my mother's trees in the next room. They are even more beautiful.'

'Do tell me about bonsais. I'm sorry, I know very little about them,' he asked, watching her carefully.

Shweta's eyes and face lit up with childlike enthusiasm as she began talking on her pet topic in a soft, hesitant voice, 'You see, the word "bonsai" means trees that are planted on trays or similar shallow containers. It is the art of dwarfing trees and developing them into appealing shapes with the aid of strings and wires. This art was developed in China, around AD 1000. It was originally called "pun-sai". The Chinese used to create fiery dragons and arched serpents out of bonsai trees. In Chinese imperial palaces, sometimes entire jungles were created in miniature.

'Then this form became hugely popular in Japan and later spread all over the world. The Japanese made bonsais world-famous. They added rocks, other plants, small houses and human figures to their bonsais. They called this art "bonkei". And like the Chinese, they also created entire bonsai landscapes and jungles that they called "sai-kei". The Japanese are masters at the art of landscaping.'

Rahul nodded appreciatively even as he looked around.

Shweta caressed the leaves of the trees as she continued to speak, 'Trees with small leaves make better bonsais, as do flowering plants like bougainvilleas, azaleas and fruit trees like cherries, plums, oranges and lemons. They can be grown both indoors and outdoors, but require a lot of skill and patience. The branches are clipped, pruned and wired to give the desired shape and to stunt their growth. Correct watering and fertilizer techniques have to be employed. Some bonsais can live up to hundreds of years just like regular trees.' She had a faraway look in her eyes. 'Unlike humans . . .' she said and then was silent.

Rahul smiled, 'Thank you Shweta. May I look at your banyan tree? I see that you've been working very hard on it.'

'Yes,' she spoke with apparent pride, 'He's older than the others.' Rahul noticed the use of "he" for the tree. It was almost as if she was talking about family. 'I started work on him when I first began work on bonsais ten years back, when my mother was alive . . .'

The banyan tree was a foot in height with an amazing number of hanging roots. It was almost like a full-grown 150-year-old banyan tree in miniature. He went to admire it at close quarters. Suddenly there was a gleam of excitement in his eyes. Three of the roots seemed to speak to him! Should he acknowledge that he had got a message? No! He slowly moved away as if he had not noticed anything, sat on a chair at the far end of the room and spoke quietly to her for some more time.

She seemed so normal, he thought, but her eyes told a different story. They had turned from friendly to disapproving to even threatening, all within the space of minutes. He carried on the conversation with kid-gloves, afraid to offend her in any way.

But careful as he was, he was shocked at the reaction he elicited when he mentioned two names. One was that of Neela for whom he already knew she had developed antipathy, and the banyan bonsai had given the other name away. Each time these names were mentioned, even casually, the reaction was startling. Then, as he was looking around, he saw a newspaper on the table with Rajeev Kabra's photo encircled with a pen.

'Do you know him?' he asked.

Shweta held out her hand for the paper and after seeing the photo, smiled. 'Yes I know him. This is Mr Kabra. He was Sunanda's friend,' she said casually.

Rahul did not know how far he could push Shweta, so he smiled back at her and said, 'He's a very famous man. You must've heard that he's a member of the cricket board?'

'Yes he told me, and he has always been very kind to me. In fact, he was one of the few people who cared for me. He also gave me some excellent advice . . .' Shweta suddenly stopped talking as if realizing she might say something she ought not to and abruptly told Rahul that he should leave.

Rahul decided not to push his luck too much. He did not want Shweta to have a relapse, so he again complimented her on her beautiful bonsais and said goodbye.

While descending the stairs, he turned around on impulse. He was startled to see her large eyes steadily following him. For a moment Rahul was unnerved. He thought that with a trishul in her hand she would have looked just like Goddess Durga!

Neela was in the living room waiting for him as she read the day's newspapers. She looked up and smiled. Was she an honest person, or a very good actress? I'm getting morbidly suspicious about people, he thought. A few more years in the police force and I'll trust no one! He shook hands with Neela, thanked her for being so accommodating and walked out.

Once outside, he got into his police jeep and suddenly felt that Act II was yet to begin in this case, and some more dramatic developments were in store. Then he mentally kicked himself for such negative thoughts. But he felt there were too many things happening too quickly and this bothered him. There was loads of work that day and no time to update his report. As he drove out he said to himself, 'I need to know where Sunanda got all that money from.' He made a note that someone had to visit her bank.

The very next day Rahul sent his inspector to Sunanda's bank to meet the manager after calling him up. The manager was very courteous and showed Sunanda's account on the computer. The inspector managed to find out that Sanjay and Neela also had a joint account there, and that Neela was the guarantor for the 1.3 crore loan that Sanjay had taken. Sanjay had put in twenty lakh of his own money. The inspector called Rahul and told him what he had found out.

'Ask the manager to take a printout of the transactions of the last three months of both the accounts and request him to keep it a secret,' Rahul instructed. He then met Ravi and updated him, 'Chief, Dr Sanjay Nanda was having an affair with Sunanda before he got married to Neela. And even after marriage I think the affair continued. Sunanda was sending ten thousand rupees a month to her parents and had also bought them a car recently. Besides this, she had built them a house that is maintained beautifully. It is the only one in the locality with a landscaped garden and is freshly painted. Someone was obviously giving her a lot of money. I also found out that Sanjay Nanda's office has cost him a whopping 1.5 crore rupees—funded by his dear wife Neela.'

'Hmm . . .' Ravi observed but said nothing.

'And I had a very fruitful day with the elder sister Shweta. She seems to have developed a dislike for her sister and a fondness for someone else. When I went near her banyan tree to admire it I saw that she had manipulated the roots to create a message! I am a bad artist but let me try to draw it for you . . .'

S ♡ S

'... what do you think?'

'There are two "Ss" with presumably a heart in between. Oh, I get it, "S loves S"!' Ravi exclaimed and Rahul smiled. 'Now who are these two "Ss"? There were three people in the house whose names began with an S: Sanjay, Shweta and Sunanda, the nurse who died. One has to be Sanjay, and the other is either Shweta or Sunanda. Since Shweta has written it, it's more likely that the message means "Shweta loves Sanjay". Have I analysed it correctly?'

'Yes, but chief it also struck me just now that it may mean "Sunanda loves Sanjay". Neela, Shweta's sister, is married to Sanjay, but Sanjay was having an affair with Sunanda that may have continued after the marriage. Suppose Shweta had found out and she wanted to punish Sunanda on behalf of her sister? Or more likely that she herself was infatuated with Sanjay and wanted to punish Sunanda for stealing Sanjay from her, even though he was married to Neela?'

'It's difficult to say Rahul, but when three women are living in a house with one man who is a handsome professional, relationships are bound to get complicated. We'll soon find out which of the two theories is right. An easy option would be to put a few more tricky questions to Shweta, but it might precipitate a relapse in her condition, so it cannot be done. Let's think about this a bit. We also have to find out if Neela had left her office between 2 and 4 p.m. on the day Sunanda died. Rahul, can you check this out?'

Rahul went to Neela's office and easily got the information he required from the register in the lobby, where every employee had to log in and out while mentioning the time. There were two guards at the entrance, to ensure compliance. He found out that Neela had logged out only at 6 p.m. on 30 August.

That left two suspects—Sanjay and Shweta—if it was a murder. The case could also be closed concluding it was an accident. Once they knew it was a murder, they had to explore the Rajeev Kabra angle and whether he had a hand in it.

That night, as Rahul finally went to bed, two pairs of eyes haunted him. One belonged to a very pretty face that was full of excitement and something else . . . perhaps a threat? He could not put his finger on it. The other pair was serene, but very sad and disturbed, wanting to say something but holding back.

Two sisters, two pairs of very different eyes trying to convey a whole lot of messages! He knew he was going to have an uneasy night.

Eleven

Meanwhile, Ravi was continuing to investigate S.N. Rao's murder. Vineet, Rao's son who was in police custody, had his lawyer with him when Ravi went to question him. He must have been handsome once, but drinking and a debauched lifestyle had taken their toll, and he had a flabby look to him with folds under his eyes. In his usual style, Ravi began the questioning session by making a statement that covered all the facts they had till date. He often used this technique to put the suspect under stress and make him more pliable.

'We know everything about your father, your family, yourself and your relationships. For the past fifteen years, you've been a cause for concern to your parents. You have run up huge debts that have been repeatedly cleared by your father. Besides overspending, you also have other vices like smoking and drinking. And there are also rumours of a mistress, but I don't want to go into that now.'

Vineet kept silent, but listened intently. Ravi continued, 'Your parents, I believe, were really fed up with your behaviour but continued to support you because of your young family. In fact, your father was concerned enough to take you to the farmhouse for a one-to-one counselling session.' Vineet looked shocked, but did not react.

'The session, we know, apparently went off well, since your father telephoned your mother to tell her that you were repentant and wanted to change. But probably it was a ploy on your part to lull your father into feeling that everything would be fine, while you were actually planning his death.'

This time Vineet looked very upset but still did not speak.

'I don't know whether you are aware of my reputation or not, but Mr Bansal, your lawyer, must know that I always get to the truth, and never give up till I do. Now I'm going to ask you some questions that I've prepared; please answer them as truthfully as you can.'

In the questions, simple everyday queries were interspersed with those relating to the murder. But Bansal had coached his client well. Vineet came out with flying colours, denying all accusations and agreeing with known facts. It was a tedious two-hour interaction for all of them, but it was not entirely a waste of time.

Astute policeman that he was, Ravi could figure out that Vineet's responses to a few questions did not ring true. To the question, 'Did you know that relations between your father and the other members of the cricket board were strained,' Vineet came out with an markedly loud and firm 'no'. Again, when Ravi asked whether Vineet himself had any dealings with the cricket board, the answer was a vehement 'of course not!'.

There was something there that needed to be investigated.

Ravi wound up the session, 'I'm disappointed that you have not answered many of my questions truthfully. We'll end today's session now, but you will soon realize that it is always better to tell the truth, otherwise things can get unpleasant later.'

To the waiting media, which had gathered outside, Ravi as usual maintained his reticence, saying firmly that he would issue a statement at the right time. Vineet, however, proclaimed his innocence to them.

Ravi was still pondering over his discussion with Vineet when he received a call from his friend and forensic expert, Madhukar Gupta. 'Ravi, I have the details of the post-mortem and other reports. Would you like to come over?'

'Of course!' Ravi immediately got up to leave.

When he reached Gupta's hospital, the detailed post-mortem and chemical analysis reports were on his friend's table. The familiar stench of formaldehyde pervaded the room, since Madhukar was still wearing his overalls.

'I'll first tell you about the post-mortem report. As I had already indicated while conducting the examination, the body showed evidence of asphyxia, er . . . effects of oxygen deprivation. There was congestion of lungs, kidneys and brain, but this could be due to many causes. There was no clear indication of acute myocardial infarction, or heart attack in common language, although the heart did show evidence of oxygen deprivation. There was also no evidence of cerebral thrombosis, or haemorrhage, like a clot or bleeding in the brain that could have caused sudden death. Chemical analysis of body fluids like urine, saliva, sweat, gastric juice and bile has also come out negative. Among poisons, such a picture in my experience can point to a poison called Aconite. Let me tell you about it . . .'

Ravi listened carefully.

'Aconite, my dear friend, is a cheap, easily available poison that can be disguised in an edible substance like alcohol or paan. Its taste is easily camouflaged and the body quickly destroys it leaving no residue. Aconite is called the "monk's hood", or locally as mitha zehar, and is freely available in the Himalayan regions. From there, it is procured and used all over the country mainly as cattle poison. All parts of the plant are poisonous, but the roots especially so. In humans, it first stimulates, and then depresses the nervous system. What happens is that the patient first has an intense sweet taste in his mouth, then there is severe burning in the throat and stomach, followed by salivation, vomiting and diarrhoea. He quickly becomes dehydrated and weak. There is profuse sweating and the body temperature falls. This is followed by muscle twitching, cramps, fall in blood pressure, slowing down of pulse. Convulsions soon follow, ultimately ending in paralysis. Death is due to depression of heart and respiration.'

'And how much quantity of this drug is needed to kill a man?'

'Two hundred and fifty milligrams of the extract of the plant, twenty-five drops of the pure tincture, or one-two grams of the root are fatal within two to six hours of intake. The patient, however, remains conscious almost till the end.'

'Madhukar, what do you think happened in this case?' Although it was clear to Ravi what had happened, he still wanted to hear the professional opinion.

'I am nearly certain that aconite was the poison chosen, and you must carry out your investigation presuming so. Another hint, find out if the minister had had paan or alcohol the night he died and who gave it to him. Also send someone to the farmhouse as soon as possible to look for any discarded container that may have carried the poison.'

'Thanks Madhukar, we've already found out that he was served paan that night, and we've also been to the farmhouse, found some containers and sent them to the forensic lab.'

'Good thinking Ravi, with your intelligence and experience, you don't need to be told much! Let me know if you require any other information. Rao was a good man victimized needlessly, and I hope he gets justice.'

By the time Ravi left the hospital, it was late in the

evening. A lot of questions were clouding his mind but he knew they would have to wait until the next day when he would get a chance to speak to Rao's family.

~

The next day when Ravi reached Rao's home to question his family, Anu and Dilip were there to receive him and said that the rest of the members would join them later. Ravi had already run a background check on all of them. His men had been working overtime gathering all the information they could and Rahul had written out their profiles. He would begin with questioning Dilip and Anu.

Ravi smiled at this beautifully matched couple. They really seemed to be made for each other. Dilip himself was not handsome in the regular sense but had immense charisma, while Anu was delicately beautiful. He turned to Dilip, 'What made you suspect that your father-in-law's death was not a natural one? You told us a little the other day. Can you elaborate some more?'

Dilip was more than happy to. 'Well, it was not one incident or two. In subtle ways we were given the message that we were not on the same wavelength as the other members of the board. Especially after the Surya—TLI— episode when we openly voiced our dissent, they did not like it. There had been a tacit agreement that all members of the board would support common decisions, no matter what. We did go along with them every time, but my father-in-law had voiced his misgivings and I supported him and that was not to their liking. I had started to get the feeling that we were being excluded from many confidential meetings. And then my father-in-law told me about something that he had discovered. Unaccounted money received as kickbacks was being siphoned off towards funding a major opposition party. And I also received an anonymous call warning me to keep away from him. Things kept adding up, making me very uneasy, and I expected the worst.'

'Anuji, did you notice any change in your father before this tragedy?' Ravi asked, turning to the daughter.

'No, he was very good at keeping his problems to himself and especially with me he always presented a happy front. My mother might've noticed something since she spent more time with him. Another thing I want to add: I do not know who killed my father and how, but as a sister I feel it could not be my brother. However bad he is otherwise, I do not think he killed him.'

'I'm sorry, but we have to go by the book and retain him in police custody. But we will release him as soon as we are able to confirm his innocence. You may move a bail petition if you so wish. Well, that's all from both of you. Now I'd like to talk to the rest of your family and Rao sir's driver.'

When Ravi saw Indu, he was impressed by her apparent poise and composure. Her husband's death and her son's recent arrest must have affected her badly, but she did not show it.

'Madam, I would like to ask you a few questions if it is all right.'

'Please go ahead. I'll answer to the best of my ability.'

They were sitting in the large, spacious and immaculately kept living room of the house. Mrs Rao seemed to have exceptional taste and Ravi could see art objects and expensive articles in practically every corner. Tea arrived in a silver tray and dainty bone china cups. Ravi waited till the domestic help had served them and vanished behind the curtains.

He cleared his throat and asked, 'I want to know about your conversations with your husband when you were in the US.'

'Our conversations were of the normal kind regarding his health, whether he was taking his medications regularly, eating on time, feedback regarding the rest of the family, etc.,' she responded.

'Tell me about his relationship with Vineet, your elder son.'

She looked a little disturbed this time. 'His relationship with my elder son was bad, for which I blame mainly Vineet. Both of us have had a tough time handling him and his problems. We thought that marriage would make him more responsible, but that did not happen, and his wife Mala has had to suffer a lot because of it. We have supported him in every way we could, but I'll not deny that there were serious arguments between father and son. In fact, it seemed to have been getting worse recently, so when my husband called me from the farmhouse to say that the counselling session with Vineet had gone off very well, I was relieved.'

'Hmm ... What about his opinion regarding the other members of the cricket board? You must have heard your son-in-law voice his suspicions.'

'I did get the feeling that there were serious issues between my husband and some members of the board, and that my husband was not acknowledging them. I even suggested once that if he felt morally responsible for joint decisions which he did not like, he should quit. I think he did have some such plan in mind but the problem was that he was probably privy to a number of secrets, and they could not let him leave easily.'

Ravi leaned forward, 'Did he name any specific member of the board?'

'No, he did not think it was ethical to do so.'

'What about his relations with Dilip and your personal opinion of your son-in-law?'

'All of us get along very well with Dilip, especially my husband who had begun to regard him as his chief confidant and right-hand man. I feel he is the most dependable son-in-law that I could have got and I am proud of him.'

'One last question madam, who do you think was responsible for your husband's death?'

She spoke slowly, 'Who could be behind his death I really don't know. My heart tells me it couldn't be Vineet. And I am also extremely shocked that *anyone* could want to do away with such a gentle and God-fearing person like my husband.' Tears appeared in her strained eyes as she lost her tightly held composure for a moment.

Ravi attempted to relax her, 'Maybe, madam, that was the reason. Maybe he was too straightforward for people's liking.' He finished his tea and said, 'Thank you madam, you have been very helpful. I promise you that we'll do our best to get to the bottom of this case and release Vineet at the earliest if he is not guilty.' Then he requested to see all of Rao's emails, 'I want to see if there were any significant ones that may help us in solving the case.'

'Please come, I know the diary in which he had noted important information. It will probably have his IDs and passwords. I'll show them to you.'

'I would like to quickly finish talking to the rest of the family members and then go with you if you don't mind.'

She nodded, 'You can ask anyone to call me when you're done.'

Anu's younger sister Priya was a perky teenager and clearly disliked her elder brother for the bad name he was bringing to the family, and unhesitatingly said so. Regarding the cricket board, she said she did not know enough about them to comment on. She'd always been a great fan of Dilip's and was thrilled to have him as a brother-in-law. As to who was behind her father's death, she said she could not say but was not prepared to exonerate her brother like her sister and mother.

Rao's younger son Hari was like his parents—simple and God-fearing. He was not as outspoken as his sisters and also did not have a strong antipathy towards his elder brother. Regarding the cricket board, he too did not have any clear-cut opinion, although like his sister, he hero-worshipped Dilip.

The background on Vineet's wife Mala was that she came from a middle-class family, whose status was far removed from that of her husband's. She looked like a quiet and efficient woman as she entered the room; perhaps more subdued because of the recent tragic incidents of her father-in-law's death, followed by her husband's arrest.

Ravi began his questioning gently, 'Madam, tell me what you know about the events of the past week.'

'I am extremely sad at the death of my father-in-law and also upset at my husband's arrest. I think it must've been a coincidence that he died when my husband was also there. I do not think *he* could be involved in any way.' It almost sounded like a plea.

'Did your husband discuss any meetings that he had with the cricket board with you?' Ravi asked, almost pitying the tall, dark woman before him. He wondered how she fitted in with the rest of the family, particularly her mother-in-law, who seemed the kind of person who took charge and liked things done her way.

'My husband did not share his business dealings or his secrets with me, therefore I do not know much about them. Even about going to the farmhouse, he told me only at the last minute. In fact, I would have liked to accompany him there since I love that place, but he did not ask me,' she sighed.

'Thank you madam,' Ravi said with a smile, 'I hope things work out well for you.'

Mala gave a wan smile, nodded and walked away.

The last person Ravi had to question was Rao's driver. Ramu had been with Rao from his Hyderabad days, and like his physician and caretaker at the farmhouse, had followed him to Delhi.

'Ramu, tell me about your master,' Ravi asked as they sat in an anteroom next to the minster's office.

'Sir, to me my master was like God, and his death is an unbearable loss. In fact, I am contemplating returning to Hyderabad next month, as I do not feel like staying on here without him,' Ramu said with folded hands. He looked about sixty-ish and had a very dark complexion with slicked back, well-oiled hair.

'What do you think about his son Vineet?'

Ramu appeared troubled. 'Sir, it is difficult for me to like anyone who harassed my master. In fact, they had a very big fight recently when I was driving them, in the course of which he had even threatened to harm his father.'

Ravi was on alert immediately. 'What about the cricket board members? Do you have any knowledge of them?'

'Sir, I do not know much about them, but in the recent past, my master had been quiet and withdrawn every time he came out of the board office.' His hands were still folded.

'Do you want to tell me anything else?' asked Ravi.

'Sir, I also want to tell you that my master was very good to me. Besides my salary, he took care of my children's education, my family's health, and had even got me two insurance policies.'

Rahul thanked the driver and said he would talk to him again if needed. Then as an afterthought, he decided to question Vineet's driver too.

Vineet seemed to have changed his drivers frequently, unlike his father. Nathu was a local man from Delhi and had been working for Vineet for only a year.

'Tell me about your sahib,' Ravi asked.

'Sir, my sahib treats me well and I have no complaints. As long as I obey him he is never upset with me. But there were occasions when he would tell me that he would drive the car himself and I should stay back home. Initially, I was scared that I had annoyed him in some way, but later I learnt to accept it quietly.'

'Drive himself? Hmm, that's interesting, a minister's son driving the car himself! Do you remember the approximate dates when this happened?'

Nathu was not very educated, but as a driver he had learnt to maintain a log-book to keep track of the car's mileage. He was therefore able to produce the dates and time when Vineet had driven the car himself.

Ravi took down the details and thanked the driver. As he was about to leave, Dilip told him that Rao's personal physician had come to see Indu and if he wanted he could talk to him too. Ravi decided to do so and went back to the living room where the doctor was waiting.

Dr Reddy told Ravi how he was shattered at his friend and mentor's death and would never be able to get over it.

'Dr Reddy, I have one question to ask you. Why did you presume Rao's death was a natural one even though he died suddenly? Should you not have ordered a post-mortem?'

'Rao was hypertensive with a history of epilepsy and asthma,' the doctor replied uncomfortably. 'There was every possibility of a heart attack. And I had no reason to think that the death was anything but natural and so certified it as one,' the family physician answered.

'Thank you sir, that's all for the present.'

He then asked Dilip whether Indu could see him now. Indu came to the living room with the diary and Dilip brought his laptop. They opened Rao's Yahoo and

Rediffusion mails with the help of the IDs and passwords supplied by Indu.

'Dilip, I want you to open all mails from the cricket board members in the last few months first, and then we'll scan his inbox for other seemingly suspicious mails.'

Dilip quickly scanned the inbox and found a folder marked CB which they assumed was for the cricket board. Most of the mails were routine stuff but there was an intriguing mail from Rajeev Kabra.

It read: Congratulations on the success of operation-M!

'What could operation-M mean? It is from Rajeev Kabra so it would have to be something connected to the board. It is dated 11 August ... Oh! I have it, M-Mane.

'Mr Mane died on 11 August. I remember the date because he died on Anu's birthday!' Dilip exclaimed.

'But why congratulate your father-in-law on Mane's death?' Ravi asked.

'As you say, why send such a mail to my father-in-law who was a known friend of the former treasurer? Could there be another meaning to it? It is very confusing and does not make sense to me too,' Dilip replied.

None of the other mails was of significance in his other accounts.

At last Ravi said, 'Dilip, please forward this mail to my email ID. Also, take a printout of this if you can. By the way, can you come with me to the police station? Rahul should be there, and the three of us may together make something of this. He is smarter than me when it comes to computers. I somehow feel it might be important.'

'Sure,' Dilip responded, 'Let me forward the mail to both of you, so that we can take a printout in your office.' Then shutting down the laptop he said, 'Okay, I'm done, let's leave.'

They got into Ravi's jeep and made their way to the police headquarters where they headed straight for Rahul's office. Ravi briefed him about the day, concluding with the email from Rajeev Kabra which they had found in Rao's account.

'Well,' said Rahul, '"Congratulations on the success of operation-M" can mean various things. Now that Mane, if "M" actually stands for him, as is most likely, is no more, he ceases to be a future threat to them, therefore the congratulations. But why the word "operation"? Did they have a hand in his death—is that possible?

'And also chief, something just occurred to me. Suppose this mail was *not* meant for Rao? It was meant for, say, someone else in the board? Which seems more likely to me. The mail was composed first and then the address added, and when clicking, by oversight it may've been sent to him, since all the board IDs are probably—and we'll have to confirm this—stored next to each other on Kabra's computer under the CB group name. Let me show you how this can happen. Rajeev Kabra has his contact list neatly arranged in different address groups, and his CB group has the contacts arranged something like this—

xyz@rediff.com
abc@yahoo.com
snrao@yahoo.com

'Now, suppose, instead of clicking on the ID of the intended recipient, he accidentally clicked on Rao's and sent it? I also organize my contacts similarly and make the same mistake sometimes and want to recall the mail afterwards, but I believe it cannot be done.'

'Brilliant Rahul! That is one possibility,' Ravi beamed at Rahul. Dilip too smiled. Ravi completed the picture, 'And continuing that chain of thought, suppose they had a hand in the death of Mane and the "operation" was a success; then

Rajeev Kabra accidentally sends a congratulatory mail to Rao instead of to the intended board member. And the message appears on his screen: Your mail has been successfully sent to the following person—*snrao@yahoo.com*—*already a contact.*'

'Yes chief, that would've driven Rajeev Kabra into a tizzy!'

'Now how would he react? Here is S.N. Rao, already objecting to their style of functioning and possessing quite a bit of inside knowledge about their activities, and he receives this dangerous mail. The people involved know that Rao is smart enough to come to the correct conclusion. They already want to ease him out, but now it will have to be permanent. What do you think Dilip?'

'I am absolutely fascinated and impressed by the way you two work and how your minds operate at the same wavelength,' Dilip replied, smiling.

'Dilip, when two people work closely together for a length of time this is bound to happen,' Ravi answered.

'Well, I think you guys have analysed things beautifully, and knowing the concerned parties, you may be correct. In fact, like I said earlier, I have been bothered that there wasn't enough reason to murder my father-in-law, but this changes everything! If they actually had a hand in Mr Mane's death, and by mistake gave a hint of it to my father-in-law, they would definitely have felt threatened enough to eliminate him.'

'But coming to Rao himself, how would he have reacted to such a mail?'

Dilip answered, 'I think he would've felt that they could not have had a direct hand in Mr Mane's death. He must have thought they were referring to the psychological effect they had on him that led to a heart attack. He would've also felt that there was enough bad blood between him and the other members of the board, and there would be no point in telling the latter that the mail was in bad taste. He must have decided to just keep quiet. Had he felt that Mr Mane's death was unnatural after receiving this mail, he would've told either me or my mother-in-law about it.'

'The problem is that Mane, who was supposed to have died of a "heart attack", was cremated the very next day after the body was flown to his home state. We'll have to see whether we can gather any evidence now. Let's try to figure out where he died and whether we can still find out something,' said Ravi.

Dilip stood up, 'Thank you guys. I know you will get to the bottom of this. We also need to trace out who the mail was really intended for. I'll take your leave now.'

After he had left, Ravi turned to his junior, 'Rahul, if you are done with the South Delhi murder investigation, find out where Mane died and any details that are available. I suspect something bigger here.'

'I'll put someone on the job. Meanwhile, we need to look into the other murder case that Ajay Shukla told us may have a connection with the Rao case.'

Twelve

Rahul and Ravi were sitting in Ravi's office to go through the documents of the second murder the Ex-el TV channel reporter Ajay Shukla had led them to.

'Chief,' said Rahul, 'the second case Ajay mentioned is the death of a woman in a medical college. Let me read it out to you.'

'The two principal people involved in this case are Dr Arvind Agarwal and his wife Rupali. Rupali Agarwal died of burns on 20 August and her husband has been arrested for it. Shall I run through it fast, or do you want me to give you the main facts?'

'Since you've taken the trouble to write it, I'll listen even as I am completing this report,' Ravi answered.

'Okay,' Rahul continued, more than happy to share his literary effort, 'So Arvind Agarwal was born thirty-five years ago to a lawyer couple who had three children. Being the youngest and the only son, he was naturally pampered to the hilt not only by his parents, but also by his sisters, who were much older to him. Arvind did not bother much with studies as a child or during adolescence, preferring to enjoy life thoroughly. From high school onwards, he had a string of girlfriends that he kept changing. Later, he also picked up some vices like smoking and drinking while at college—

seems to be a carbon copy of Vineet! His doting parents, however, never pressurized him into working hard or changing his lifestyle. But luckily for him, he was intelligent and secured enough marks to get into medicine and also managed to do an MD in biochemistry. This earned him a lecturer's post in a medical college . . .'

An urgent call from the commissioner interrupted Rahul's flow. He wanted the report Ravi was writing immediately. Ravi quickly completed it and mailed it.

'Okay, now since that's done, I can listen with full concentration. Go on Rahul,' Ravi said, relaxing on the chair a bit.

'Dr Agarwal is charming and witty, so it is natural that women are attracted to him. He had also been a university-level cricket player and was coaching the college team. This gave him additional popularity in the college.'

'He played cricket? That's interesting! Go on.'

'A few years back he got married to a pretty woman who was also slim and attractive. His wife Rupali, the person who died, was a lecturer of physics in a city college.

'Born to middle-class working parents, who were both government servants, Rupali was one of four sisters. Although she was very intelligent, being the eldest, she did not opt for any professional course since she felt it would be a financial burden on her parents. After her MSc, she took up a lecturer's post in a college and also gave tuitions, so that her earnings could supplement her parents' income and help educate her three younger sisters. She made sure that all of them entered medical college. She was thirty years old by the time she felt that her sisters could manage by themselves and she could afford to get married. Accordingly, her parents looked around. But even before they seriously set about trying, Arvind Agarwal saw her at a relative's wedding and was interested to marry her. Since his family was good and he was of their caste, Rupali's parents were only too happy to get them married,' Rahul paused for breath.

He began again, 'The marriage between Dr Agarwal and Rupali was an arranged one, but they seemed to be very fond of each other. They were always seen together after working hours, at parties or walking in the campus. Rupali continued to teach physics in a prestigious college and was also giving tuition to Rajeev Kabra's daughter at their residence.

'The couple gelled so well together that for some time, Dr Agarwal also stopped his philandering. But a year went by and old habits resurfaced. He used to smoke and drink surreptitiously behind Rupali's back, but now started doing so openly. He had also never been a one-woman man, and his extramarital liaisons resumed. Besides everything else, he was also a spendthrift and blew away all his money, so the marriage continued to go downhill.'

'Anyone else staying with them or they stayed alone?' Ravi asked.

'The couple stayed alone, chief. Arvind's family lives out of the campus.'

'Were there any servants working in the house?'

'Yes, but only a part-time woman who cleaned up the house in the evening.'

'Okay, continue.'

'Sometimes raised voices were heard from their home but the neighbours reasoned that all couples had an occasional spat, and left them alone. Then slowly people noticed that he was going around during lunch hours with an attractive intern. Being a close-knit campus with an active grapevine, word must have reached his wife. Now relations were visibly seen to deteriorate. From then on they were rarely seen outside together and raised voices inside the house became the norm. Arvind had also become more brazen about his relationship with his girlfriend.'

'Did Rupali have any friends in the campus?'

'No, she seemed to have been a workaholic keeping pretty much to herself. Except for the immediate neighbours, she did not seem to have had the time to make friends.'

'That's interesting . . .' Ravi mused.

'Over the years, Rupali slowly became more and more withdrawn and quiet. Sometime before her death she also lost the lucrative tuition assignment at Rajeev Kabra's house.'

'Wait a minute, she lost the assignment just before her death. This could be significant.'

'Yes chief, it struck me too,' Rahul answered. 'Losing the assignment made her even more depressed. Her neighbours in the campus knew that she was all alone; she was not close to her in-laws and would not trouble her own family. Then an accident happened on the morning of 20 August, when many of the staff members in the medical college campus were out on their morning walk. There was a commotion near the C-type flats. Someone had got burnt and a crowd had gathered there. Then people came to know that it was Rupali, wife of Dr Agarwal. Somebody smothered her flames with a blanket and she was rushed to the ICU. She never came out of her coma and died in two days. The general verdict in the campus was one of anger and disgust at Dr Agarwal's behaviour since they were sure he had set his wife on fire, but he kept proclaiming his innocence and behaved as if he was shattered. However, he was arrested and sent into police custody for fifteen days, which is likely to be further extended for another fifteen days.

'It seemed an open and shut case of a husband who had set his wife on fire, but Arvind Agarwal's parents are famous criminal lawyers and will not give up easily. They are determined to prove that their son is not a murderer. Arvind himself keeps saying he is innocent. He said his wife had taken her own life since she was depressed.'

'Interesting, she was giving tuitions at Rajeev Kabra's house and had lost the assignment sometime before her death. And Arvind Agarwal played university-level cricket. Is there a site-report?' Ravi asked.

'Yes, here it is, this is what the report says—It was early morning and Rupali had been set on fire when she was entering the kitchen with the milk. There was milk all over the floor, with the empty vessel lying on the ground. There was also a thin rope lying in a corner.'

'Is that all?'

'Yes chief, that's all in this case.'

All the while Rahul had been speaking, Ravi had been writing his own conclusions in a diary.

— Rupali dies of burns—murder or suicide?
— If murder—husband killed her? Any other likely suspect with access to her?
— Arvind Agarwal? He's a spendthrift, philanderer, has a bad reputation, only suspect. Parents are criminal lawyers; he has two younger sisters.
— Actions to be taken:
  Examine the couple's house; talk to Rupali's and Arvind's family, the neighbours and the department colleagues. We must also get Arvind to confess and investigate the Rajeev Kabra connection.

Rahul interrupted him, 'Oh by the way, chief, I have also received details on Mane's death. Boss, he died early morning on 11 August, at his house in Delhi. The inspector spoke to the chowkidar who lives there in the outhouse. The only person present in the house the previous night was his servant Vijay Kumar, who is not available for interrogation as he has left for his hometown Lucknow and is settled there now. But Mane's cousin had sent his cook that day to prepare dinner and according to him the guests were Ramesh Patel of Ex-el TV and Surya Seth. He also says that he cooked dinner, cleaned up and left. When he left, Mane was fine and only Vijay Kumar was with him inside the house. I also found out that some alcohol was consumed that night, and that Mane did not eat paan.'

'Then we need to get this Vijay Kumar to Delhi. Do you have his address?'

'Yes boss, and I've already sent a police party to unearth him and bring him to Delhi. I've also requested Dr Sobti, the doctor who certified Mane's death, to come here in the morning if he can. He said he would come and should be here any minute.'

'Good thinking Rahul,' Ravi said, and just as he was speaking there was a message saying Dr Sobti had arrived and was waiting for them in Rahul's office. Ravi and Rahul called him over. Sobti shook hands with them and took the seat in front of Ravi while Rahul stood with his arms folded across his chest.

Ravi said, 'Dr Sobti, thank you for coming. We want you to tell us everything you remember about the 11th of August when you were called in to certify Mr Mane's death.'

'I'd like to know the reason why you're questioning me before I answer,' Sobti was still smiling but his voice was firm.

'It's a routine legal matter in the family that has turned up for which we need to find out exactly how Mr Mane died,' Ravi answered. There was something in Ravi's demeanour that forced the doctor to cooperate.

'As far as I recollect, I got a call around 7 a.m., informing me that Mr Mane had passed away and that I should come and certify his death. I reached there by 7.30 a.m. and went to the room in which the death had occurred. I had attended to him on an earlier visit about six months back, when I'd come to know that he suffered from diabetes and high blood pressure. At that time, his blood pressure was moderately raised, and his blood sugar was also out of control, but his ECG was normal. I had adjusted his medication and given him a sedative.

'On the 11th early morning when I examined the dead body as per protocol, I found that he'd died at least four hours back as rigor mortis, the stiffening of the body, had set in. There did not seem any sign of struggle. And except for a smell of vomit that hung around the body, there was no other significant observation I could make.

'By now, some relatives and friends had arrived. I had no hesitation in certifying the death caused probably due to a massive heart attack and explained things to them. I knew they would require me to fill up a form later, and asked them to come to my clinic for it. After that I left the house.'

'Do you remember who these "relatives and friends" were?'

Sobti thought for a moment. 'One was supposed to be a cousin. The others I do not know.'

'Dr Sobti, I'm going to ask you a tricky question—is it usual for a doctor to issue a death certificate when the circumstances under which a person died are not known?'

The doctor shifted uncomfortably in his chair. 'I go by my gut instinct. In this case I knew he was a patient of hypertension and diabetes that were not well under control, and he also led a stressful life. Such a person is usually at a high risk of a heart attack. And I had no reason to think otherwise. Are you suspecting foul play?' He looked a bit nervous now.

'We don't know as yet. We are still conducting investigations,' Ravi answered, standing up. 'Thank you for your time doctor. We may get back to you again.'

~

Two days later, Ravi got a call from the police party that had been sent to Lucknow. They said they'd got Vijay Kumar and that they would be reaching with him by train in the morning by 11 a.m. As soon as Vijay Kumar arrived, he was locked up without food or drink for several hours. Ravi purposely did not meet him that day and told the personnel not to let him sleep peacefully.

When Ravi called Vijay Kumar to his interrogation room the next day, the latter was extremely nervous and shivering with fright. Vijay saluted Ravi and stood shaking in terror. Ravi knew that his condition had made him easier to handle. Rahul also came in and sat silently on the chair next to Ravi.

The interrogation room was small and furnished with the bare minimum. It had a table and three chairs and was rather dimly lit except for the prisoner's chair which was brightly lit up with an overhanging bulb.

Since they knew how S.N. Rao had been killed, Ravi suspected that the same plan would have been first tried out on Mane, who had died before, and then replicated on Rao.

Without giving the suspect any time to relax, Ravi began in his trademark style, 'We have brought you here to question you about the death of Mr Mane with whom you had been working. On the night of 10 August, you were in Mr Mane's house as a servant. At night he and two of his friends had dinner with drinks after which the guests left. The cook who had come to prepare dinner, also left.

'After that Mr Mane probably asked for a drink again and you served him. But before entering the room, you emptied out the contents of a small bottle into the glass. This bottle was given to you by someone who has told us about it. After serving the drink you somehow managed to take away his mobile phone and locked the door from outside when you were leaving, so that your master could not escape or call for help. Then you coolly went off to sleep.'

Vijay Kumar had begun to sweat profusely now and was barely able to keep himself under control. Ravi noticed the reaction, but continued his narrative as if he had not seen anything, 'A few hours later, you quietly unlocked his door and looked in. He was on the bed and seemed dead. You kept his mobile back and went to bed again. In the morning you called Dr Sobti who came and certified the death as probably due to a heart attack. You had also phoned some local relatives who took away the body.'

Ravi paused, let the suspense build up further, then resumed, 'You collected the large amount of money that you were promised from the person who had hired you and went back to Lucknow. But recently we have been investigating another murder and we came to know that Mr Mane's death was not a natural one. During the investigation we also found out that you were responsible for your master's death.'

Vijay Kumar had guilt written all over his face. *The police seemed to know everything!*

He immediately spilled the beans, 'Sahib, I did not know what effect the liquid would have, otherwise I would never have done it.'

Rahul was elated at the response, but had learnt to control his emotions like his boss. Ravi continued in a matter of fact tone, 'How much money did you receive?'

The man kept quiet.

Ravi leaned forward and spoke in a slow, menacing tone, 'Vijay, you are already in deep shit since we know of your role in the murder. You may even get a death sentence, as it was you who put the poison in that drink. But if you give a truthful statement, you may get a lesser sentence.'

Vijay Kumar was now trembling from head to foot. He had never thought that he would be caught, but when the police had come looking for him he had immediately known the reason. He was already in a state of partial breakdown, his shameful arrest in front of his family, the long train journey under police escort, the lack of food and water and sleep had all taken their toll on him. It did not take much to 'persuade' him to make a statement.

'On the morning of 10 August, I was approached by a man wearing dark glasses and a muffler outside the Renaissance hotel where I had been called to meet him. He told me of a plan and said I would get a huge amount of money if I played my part right. All I had to do was put the liquid he gave me into my master's drink. The man knew that two people would come and meet my master for dinner and that after dinner he would order a glass of Bloody Mary for himself. In fact, he seemed to know everything about my master.'

'Wait a minute, were you approached by a short, fat sardar who came in a white Zen a few days earlier, asking you about Mr Mane's plans and his eating and drinking habits?' Ravi guessed that Arora of Ace Detective Agency would've been hired for the job.

Vijay Kumar looked stunned, 'Yes sir, he asked me a few questions and gave me two hundred rupees. He said he was a journalist and was going to write about my master.'

'And you agreed to give all the details? Okay, continue with your statement.'

Vijay Kumar looked apologetic and was in a pathetic state by now. 'All I had to do was to put the liquid in his drink. Sahib always had a night cap of Bloody Mary whenever he stayed here, so I decided I would put the liquid into that. But I was told to buy two paans and keep them in readiness, in case he did not ask for the drink. I had to put the liquid into the paans and persuade him to have them. And I had to take away his mobile and lock the door from outside. At that time I did not realize the implication of it all. I did everything as per instructions, but I did not know, sahib, that he would die!'

'Where is the bottle that contained the liquid, what did you do with it?'

Vijay Kumar looked totally crushed now, 'Sahib, I was told to dispose it off safely, but felt no one would find out, so I just threw it into the dustbin in the master bedroom.'

Ravi gave Rahul a significant look—they could still find some evidence!

'How much money did you receive?'

With great deal of difficulty, Ravi was able to elicit the fact that Vijay had received five lakh rupees for the part he had played.

'You mean to say that you received that kind of money and still believed that the liquid you put in the drink would not kill your master?' Rahul now took over the interrogation.

Vijay Kumar looked down without speaking, his remorse coming to the surface.

'Who gave you the money and how?'

'I had booked my ticket to Lucknow and was handed over the bag with the money at the railway station. He was a tall man dressed in a driver's uniform.'

'Where is the money now?'

'Still in the bag at home, I was planning to buy a one-room tenement in Lucknow with it and have been looking out for one.'

'Anything else you want to tell us?'

Vijay Kumar just kept quiet. He was totally drained.

'Would you recognize the person who gave you that bottle if you saw him?'

'I . . . I'm not sure sahib.'

'But you would know him if you heard his voice, right?'

The man looked startled. 'He had a very rough and grating voice sahib,' he answered.

Ravi told his men to formally arrest Vijay Kumar.

That evening, Ravi held an update session with Rahul. 'Chief, it just struck me that we started off investigating one murder, but thanks to a series of coincidences we are unravelling several others. I just get the feeling that before we end, we'll have more bodies piling up!'

'Rahul, the time for gory jokes will come later. We still have a lot of work to do.'

Rahul grinned, 'Sorry chief, the thought just came to my head and I spoke it out loud.'

'To be honest, that's exactly what I felt too, but I think we'll soon put a stop to all this. Rahul, go to the house and do a spot inspection and check out the dustbin. This stupid man just threw the bottle and escaped without thinking of the consequences. If we're lucky, it may still have not been emptied.'

Ravi was right; since the house had been locked soon after the death the dustbin had not been emptied and the container was still there. Rahul did not find anything else of consequence and sent the container to the forensic lab.

∼

Ravi was following up on the Rupali murder case. He went to the medical college campus in civil clothes. The police personnel who had initially attended the call had already examined the flat where Arvind and Rupali lived. It was locked up now. Ravi was more interested in the general ambience and in understanding the psychology of the occupants than in collecting evidence. He opened the flat and entered. The smell of kerosene and burnt clothes still hung in the air but the house had been cleaned after the police panchnama. He switched on the lights, opened the windows, tied his kerchief around his nose and started going through the flat. A thought came to him that just a few weeks back this was a 'home' to people and now, after the tragedy, it was only the 'scene of crime'.

The house was neat and clean, and the general impression he got was one of orderliness and quiet elegance. The entrance led to the drawing room and from there to the kitchen on the right side. There was no door between the drawing room and the kitchen. If you walked straight from the entrance without turning right towards the drawing room or kitchen, a corridor led to a tiny study with attached bathroom and further ahead into the master bedroom with another attached bathroom.

This bedroom had a small balcony.

Rupali's clothes were in the cupboards of this bedroom and Arvind's in the small study room. Arvind's room had a liquor cabinet that was well-stocked with foreign liquor and expensive brands of cigarettes. Ravi was surprised to notice that there were also more scent bottles, after-shave lotions, hair gels and cosmetics in Arvind's room than in Rupali's. Each had a study table in their room that Ravi examined in detail, but did not find anything worth noting except a latest edition, slim desktop PC on Arvind's study table.

He went through the flat thoroughly but couldn't find any incriminating evidence.

As he was leaving the flat, Ravi thought that Arvind Agarwal had very expensive tastes that could not have been sustained on the earnings of two lecturers. *Were his parents giving him money, or was he borrowing from somewhere?* Most likely it was the latter. He decided to check his bank and credit card accounts, and get the official police hacker to examine Arvind's files and mail accounts on his computer for any leads.

Ravi then headed to interview the immediate neighbour. The flat complex C-1 that Arvind and Rupali were staying in had three other lecturers living in it. Dr Desai was a lecturer in anatomy and their immediate neighbour, as he lived in the flat opposite theirs. The other two lecturers lived in the flats downstairs. Desai had left for the college, but his wife and two-year-old son were at home. Ravi spoke to her in detail and she seemed very forthcoming.

She told Ravi that they had known Arvind since his wild bachelor days. When he got married they thought he had changed, but after some time he went back to his old ways and his wife Rupali became distant and withdrawn. The couple didn't seem to be on very good terms with Arvind's parents. She also spoke about their fights and how they often heard them arguing.

Ravi asked her about Rupali's work, 'Did she tell you anything about her tuition job with Rajeev Kabra's daughter?'

'Yes, she did tell me that she had lost that assignment and was looking out for a similar one.'

'Did she mention any reason for losing the assignment?'

'No.'

'Now tell me what you know about her death.'

'Well,' she sighed, 'the day Rupali died, we were busy at home with our morning routine. Suddenly there was a commotion and a lot of noise in the Agarwal residence. My husband rushed out to see what the matter was and I followed him. The door was open and we saw a dishevelled Dr Agarwal pretending to smother the flames that had engulfed Rupali. I noticed that there was spilt milk on the floor, with an empty vessel also lying there. Dr Jain and Dr Mishra who live in our building had also heard the commotion and came to help. They tore off her burning clothes and wrapped her in a blanket. Dr Jain then quickly got out his car and we carried Rupali down and drove her straight to the CCU. Treatment was immediately started, but she soon slipped into a coma and passed away.

'I was highly traumatized by the whole incident and especially about Rupali's fate. I hope Dr Agarwal will be convicted for her death as I am sure he set her on fire. He had even gagged her and tied her hands from behind before committing the crime. It was horrible!'

Ravi was instantly alert. 'How do you know she had been gagged and tied? Did you tell the police about this?'

'No,' she hesitated. 'I was very upset at that time and wasn't able to recall everything . . . But later, I remembered that it was a thin, red, cotton towel that had been used to gag her. Dr Agarwal removed it from her face in front of us. I am sorry I forgot to mention it to the police—we are normal people you know,' she added in her defence.

'Of course,' Ravi smiled reassuringly, 'Anything else you noticed?'

'Yes, there was also a thin rope lying on the floor. On seeing it I thought he must have used it to tie her hands and probably untied them when he heard us coming.'

'Can you give a signed statement stating this?'

'I will surely do so for Rupali's sake,' she gave a wan smile.

'Ma'am, you will have to come to the police station at your convenience to sign the statement. I will make sure you are not kept waiting. And thank you, your statement will be very useful.'

Ravi made a mental note to check whether the thin red towel and rope were collected by the police as evidence.

Ravi's next stop was Arvind's bank. His account was with the State Bank of India branch at the college itself. There he found out that he also held an SBI credit card from which he had borrowed heavily. He had not been able to repay his loan to the bank, but was able to remain afloat because of intermittent cash deposits into his account. *Where did these come from? If someone was giving him money, who was it?* His mounting debts could also have been a bone of contention between Arvind and Rupali, thought Ravi.

Ravi also went over to Arvind's department of biochemistry. Most of the doctors and staff were women and this was one place where Arvind got a good rating. The general consensus was that he was competent, a good teacher and a jovial person to work with. They knew about his philandering ways but were not ready to accept that he could have killed his wife. They also said that he would have tried something more subtle and refined had he wanted to kill her rather than setting her on fire. The whole department stood by him. Ravi was amused. *Was it because they were women that they had given him a positive report card?*

Meanwhile, Rahul had also been busy. He first went to interview Rupali's parents. Both the parents seemed uncomfortable at first but they soon opened up.

'We were very worried about her when she did not get married for long. However, when she was willing, we got this fantastic offer from the Agarwals. Frankly, we were a little surprised, since they are very rich people, but it seems Arvind saw Rupali at a common relative's wedding and wanted to marry her,' her mother said.

Then Rupali's father spoke, 'Everything went off well, and Rupali always told us that she was very happy. She used to come home frequently, but for the past two months her visits had become rare. However, she phoned regularly and her sisters used to visit her often. Especially Sonali, my second daughter, who is studying in the same medical college, met her almost every week. Arvind rarely came here, but we met him at functions at his parents' house and he was always very respectful towards us. On 20 August, when we got the news, we were shattered.' Then he got up, came to Rahul and grasped his hands tightly, 'You must promise to find out the truth; we are poor people and cannot employ expensive lawyers. And my daughter was not the type to commit suicide.'

Rahul was moved, 'I'll try my best, sir.' He turned to Rupali's mother, 'Mrs Sinha, did you have a doubt as to whether your daughter was unhappy in any way?'

'No, I knew my daughter; even if she had some problem due to which she was unhappy, she would not have bothered us. She never ever told us of her troubles even as a child, she would reveal only things which would make us happy.' She cried quietly as she said this.

He then spoke to Rupali's sisters, Sonali, Deepali and Swarali. Sonali was slightly plump, but very nice looking. She was doing her MD in medicine in the same college where Arvind was teaching. Deepali looked more the studious type, maybe because of her glasses, but was also attractive. She was in the final year of MBBS in another famous college in Delhi. But it was Swarali the youngest who was the prettiest. She was in second year medicine in the same college as Deepali.

Rahul introduced himself, 'Hi. I'm ACP Rahul Singh and I am investigating your sister's death. Please tell me about her and what you know about it.' He tried to be polite and careful about not hurting their feelings.

Deepali seemed the spokesperson and began, 'To us, Rupali was next to God. She was everything to us, and if she has been killed by her husband like we think she was, he should be severely punished. The Agarwals are very rich and powerful people and behaved a little condescendingly towards our parents. That hurt us because we had given away our gem to them. If you had met and interacted with Rupa, ACP Singh, you would understand what I mean.' She then turned to Sonali and Swarali, 'You two want to add anything else?'

Sonali said, 'I used to meet her often and she seemed her usual self, but she was such a strong person that I might have missed something. She may have been careful about revealing anything that I might inadvertently pass on to our parents and cause them grief. After she lost her highly paying tuition assignment at Rajeev Kabra's house, she had more time in the evenings and we met more frequently.'

'Wait a minute, she told you about that?' Rahul interrupted.

'Yes.'

'Did she also tell you why she lost it?'

'I didn't understand it properly, but she said that one evening she had been waiting in their drawing room for Gayatri, Mr Kabra's daughter to return from an appointment, when she heard Rajeev Kabra discussing something with another man. She was sitting in a recessed alcove unseen to them. When she realized that they were discussing something private and secretive, she got up to leave, but Kabra heard the slight sound she made when she got up, and he came there. On seeing her, he asked her to go up to Gayatri's room and wait. And the next day her services were terminated without giving any reason. She was very hurt at being treated like this and said that the rich and famous behaved in any way they liked, and we had no choice but to take it.'

'Did she tell you what she had overheard?' His senses were alert now.

'I don't remember everything clearly, but she said they were plotting or had plotted to bring down a Mane and Surya Seth. She also heard them use the words "do away with" and then they mentioned some Rai ... Rao. That's when she felt that she must not eavesdrop and got up.'

Sonali's brows were creased in deep thought for some time and then she suddenly exclaimed, 'Oh my god, S.N. Rao! She was talking about S.N. Rao, the minister! I remember now. Isn't he the one who died recently and is said to have been murdered. Was that what they were discussing? And was that the reason our Rupa was killed?'

Rahul was startled at her intelligence but said, 'We are investigating all the angles, but tell me, did she mention anything else?'

'She said that she was going to forget about the whole episode, and maybe look out for another assignment like it. She was, however, bitter that Gayatri, Kabra's daughter had not supported her.'

Rahul was very excited at this information, but did not show it. Sonali continued, 'I also met Arvind frequently and he was always very charming and kind. He told me that I should come to him if I had problems in college. But after rumours of his affair with an intern started surfacing, I avoided meeting him.'

'Do you think Rupali knew about this affair?'

'If she did, she chose not to reveal anything to me. And I did not have the heart to tell her about it myself.'

Swarali did not want to add anything on her own but said she felt the same as her sisters.

Rahul thought for some time and then got up to leave. He requested the family to come to the police station at their convenience to sign the statements.

'I assure you that we will do our best to get justice for Rupali, but please do not reveal any part of our conversation to anyone till the case is solved.'

Rahul walked out pleased with the investigation. The visit had been very fruitful.

Thirteen

Ravi had taken an appointment with Arvind's parents who had agreed to see him at their office. It was conveniently located in a commercial complex, two kilometres away from the Supreme Court where they practised. The building was high-end and posh-looking, with offices and some showrooms, in which the Agarwals owned a huge five thousand square feet area on the second floor. The interiors were tastefully done up and the office itself was divided into many cabins. When Ravi reached there, the whole place was buzzing with the clicking of computers and the humming of printers in an air-conditioned ambience. The Agarwals were both criminal lawyers of some standing, but they also had some lawyers in their office practising other branches of law.

They were waiting in their cabin, which was pretty opulent by any standards. Ravi went forward and shook hands with Mr Agarwal and greeted Mrs Agarwal, who were both sitting across a large, dark mahogany table with files piled high on both sides and an open laptop before Mr Agarwal.

'I'm DCP Ravi Sharma,' he introduced himself. 'I am here to ask you a few questions regarding your daughter-in-law Rupali's recent accident and death.'

'We have already given our statements to the police,' Agarwal said curtly with his hands folded in his lap. He seemed to be in a defiant mood.

But Ravi was in the mood to extract information, and his voice was firm, 'Sir, I've taken over the case now, and if you don't mind I'd like to ask you a few questions.'

Agarwal was not very tall, but he was broad and athletic and exuded a certain power that perhaps came with his position as a renowned lawyer. He was dressed in a well-tailored suit that nearly succeeded in camouflaging his expanding waistline. But even the best tailor in town could not hide the obvious plumpness of Mrs Agarwal, who looked very uncomfortable in her pantsuit and shoes.

It was not often that Ravi felt intimidated, but this was definitely one of those moments when he felt dwarfed by Agarwal's sheer personality. He knew he was up against someone who would not give up easily. This man would probably try everything from legal tangles to bribes to get his way.

'Mr Agarwal, you know why I'm here, so without any preamble let me tell you what I want. I need to know about your relations with your son Arvind, by yours I mean both of you, and with your late daughter-in-law. I also want to know if you have any knowledge of how she died and what exactly happened.'

The lawyer put his hands on the table with the fingers splayed and leaned forward. Ravi did not fail to notice that almost all the ten fingers had rings on them with different coloured stones. He mistrusted men who wore many rings—to him it was a sign of an insecure person prone to visiting astrologers and soothsayers. Such men could be dangerous.

'DCP Sharma, I know your reputation. You don't beat around the bush, so I will not waste your time. My son may not be the best in the world, but he would never kill his wife. He smokes and drinks and flirts a little but that does not make him a murderer as the police and media are trying to portray. Rupali's death was a case of suicide and my son ran after her to try and douse the fire. I have very high-level connections and will use them all to prove my son's innocence. My wife interacted more with Rupali than I did. She will tell you about her.'

Just then tea arrived and the well-dressed attendant put individual coasters and mugs for each one. After he had left, Mrs Agarwal spoke, 'Rupali was a nice girl and I got along very well with her. Since they stayed in the campus and all of us are busy people, we could not meet as often as we liked, but whatever time I spent with her was pleasant. I felt my son and she were happy with each other. Why she committed suicide is a mystery to us too.'

Ravi asked, 'Was there anything unusual you noticed in her or your son's behaviour that you want to report.'

To this Agarwal replied, 'We thought our son is mature enough to handle his family life and we didn't interfere with it. So we don't know what was happening between the two of them. However, we stand by our son.'

Ravi knew it would be difficult to pry out any more information from these two. He replied, 'Fine, I'll take your leave. Thank you sir and thank you madam, I sincerely hope that it was a case of suicide. The truth will come out, of that I can assure you.'

Ravi looked around the office as he was leaving. You could smell money there.

In the evening Ravi and Rahul met to update each other. Ravi was especially happy to receive Sonali's statement. 'We've made a beginning in all the cases, and have some evidence that at least one member of the board is connected in some way to the murders. Rupali probably overheard Kabra and another member of the board discussing the plan to kill Rao. She did not understand the full significance of what she'd heard, but the board members were worried that she may've heard too much. Kabra removed Rupali from her tuition assignment, but probably felt it wasn't enough. They couldn't take a chance and somehow induced Arvind Agarwal to murder his wife. We know Dr Agarwal was habitually short of money, and that may've been the incentive. Then there was the added advantage of getting rid of Rupali since she must have been objecting to his clandestine affairs. But at the moment we don't have adequate evidence to prove any of this. We'll have to gather it. Also, we'll have to find out who were the other members of the board who were involved.'

'Chief, I've been thinking ... is it possible for Rajeev Kabra and his co-conspirator to act without the board president's knowledge?'

'Rahul, it is possible, but we will not rule out anything. So far we have no evidence against the board president and do not know who Kabra's co-conspirator was. Tomorrow let us confront Arvind regarding his wife's murder with what evidence we have and try to extract a confession. Even if we fail to get one, we'll approach the court day after to quash his bail appeal which is coming up. Arvind's father is a very powerful man who will try every trick in the book to get bail for his son and we have to somehow stop him. Once we ensure Arvind Agarwal does not get bail, we can find out if other members of the board were involved in any way,' concluded Ravi.

The next day when Ravi and Rahul went to meet Arvind who was in police custody, the senior Agarwal was already there with his son. They sensed that by now he would have diligently coached his son on what to say and when to keep his mouth shut. Ravi was aware he would have a tough time, but he was ready for this. In his usual style he geared up to tell Arvind the story they had prepared. But before that he turned to Arvind's father and said firmly, 'Mr Agarwal, whatever I'm going to say, I can substantiate, so please do not try to intervene in the middle or stop me. I am just going to state my case and place the evidence we have in front of you. You both can have your say later.'

He then turned to Arvind and began, 'Being good-looking and having plenty of money, you have been womanizing ever since your medical college days. You've got into frequent spats with your father for this. And by the time you had finished your MD, your relations with your father had plumbed to such depths that you had to leave home and live on the campus. Meanwhile, you also ran into debts. Someone from the family, probably your mother, continued to support you financially, even bailing you out of your credit card debts, which you got into very often because of your extravagant lifestyle.

'Thus, when you approached your parents saying you wanted to marry a simple middle-class girl, they were happy, thinking she might have a stabilizing influence on you. For some time this did happen, but a year after your marriage, you were back to your old ways. We have met your neighbours in the campus who will substantiate this. This led to a rift in your marriage which your wife tried to repair. She was a woman who had worked very hard in life to support her parents in educating her three younger sisters, and was not the sort of person who would bother them with her personal problems. Unfortunately, she could not discuss things with her in-laws either. She therefore put up a brave front and carried on as if nothing was amiss.

'When you got involved with Ms Gaur, an intern, it became the talk of the college, and there was no way your wife would not have known about it. And as you increasingly became more brazen about your relationship with your girlfriend—the rift between the two of you got wider. Rupali probably also found out the extent of your debts and threatened to approach your father. You thought you were having a good life with a girlfriend and had a supportive mother. You did not want your father to come to know that you were in debt again. And Rupali, far from being the simpleton you thought she was, had turned out to be a person with a mind of her own. You therefore planned to do away with her in a way that would look like suicide, so you set her on fire one morning. We are also exploring the possibility that someone offered you monetary inducement to carry out this crime. We will confront you with that evidence when we get the confirmation. Our sleuths are working on it.'

As soon as Ravi paused, Arvind's father spoke in a low, menacing voice that he was fighting hard to control. 'DCP Sharma, you have cooked up a nice fairy tale, but let me tell you that it won't stand up in court. I will drill so many holes in that story that by the time I'm through, you'll be left only with a sieve through which all your "evidence" will drain off. Arvind will not confess to a crime that he did not commit. It was a case of suicide and I will prove it in court! I know your reputation and I hope you know *mine*. We will see who wins. Arvind beta, I will advise you not to say anything beyond "I am not guilty"!'

Arvind did as he was told, since he was probably very scared for the first time in his life, and felt that only his father could save him.

Agarwal turned to Ravi again, 'DCP Sharma, a word of advice, you are putting your reputation at stake this time. If you know what is good for your health, you will not oppose me.'

Ravi was furious by now, 'Mr Agarwal, you take care of your own health. I know how to take care of mine! And before we conclude, chew on this fact—why did Rupali gag herself and tie her own hands from behind before supposedly "committing suicide"?'

He did not wait for an answer but walked out with Rahul after ringing the bell to call in his juniors to take Arvind away.

As they took Arvind back into custody, Agarwal walked out in deep thought, his lips pursed and his forehead creased with worry.

Ravi looked wryly at his junior, 'A very typical kind of person, Rahul, but we need not be too concerned. We'll just have to work harder to see this through. We have unsettled him a bit, but make no mistake, we are dealing with a clever opponent in the form of Arvind's father. Tomorrow we file the charge sheet, try to get his bail appeal quashed and send him to jail. I hope our friend Munir Khan will be appointed the prosecution lawyer for the state. He cannot be pressurized because he is absolutely incorruptible and we can work well as a team. We must prepare an airtight case against Arvind Agarwal, and ensure there is no leak to the press.'

Rahul had been carefully listening to his senior take on the famous lawyer. He knew he could only learn from this experience. They fell into a discussion as Ravi wanted to plug all loopholes in the case. Time was running out for them . . .

Ravi said, 'Let's explore the possibilities of Arvind's involvement in this and in the cricket board murders. The most likely connection could be that Arvind has been used by Rajeev Kabra. The second could be that Arvind Agarwal is innocent and Rupali was set on fire by someone else at Kabra's behest. The third could be that Rupali actually committed suicide which seems very unlikely, now that the neighbour has signed a statement saying that she appeared to have been gagged and bound. And the fourth possibility is that Arvind set his wife on fire on his own because she wanted to stop his philandering ways and he was in no mood to give in. We have to keep an open mind and work on all four angles. But tomorrow let's continue questioning the people on our list in the Sunanda case.'

~

Ravi went to sleep that night wondering how Kabra could, if at all, have had a hand in Rupali's death. The most likely possibility was that he felt threatened that Rupali may have overheard his conversation regarding S.N. Rao and to be on the safe side planned to eliminate her. He could have roped in Arvind and by complying with Kabra, Arvind could get rid of his wife and probably also get a bailout package to help him clear his debts.

But what bothered him was the fact that the door was open when Rupali was set on fire, the neighbour had said so. *Now why would Arvind Agarwal keep the door open while setting his wife on fire?* Or had she run to the door and opened it trying to escape, and been pulled back in by Arvind again? But her hands had been tied ... Who else could have entered the house so early in the morning, be let in by Rupali, set her on fire and leave before Arvind could come out of his bedroom? Could it have been done without Arvind's connivance or was he also involved along with someone else? All these questions kept racing through his mind and he tried to sort them out one by one, even as he slept.

By morning Ravi knew who the other suspect could be. He would send an inspector to confirm his suspicion. They would then plan on how to gather evidence and arrest the person if they were proved right!

Dr Agarwal's bail appeal hearing was to come up at 3 p.m., therefore Ravi and Rahul were at the court by 2.30 p.m. Ravi had worked very hard to make a solid case and could only hope for the best now. He was also happy that Munir Khan, an extremely competent lawyer with integrity, was the public prosecutor. There was high drama outside the court with a lot of media circus, since journalists were expecting some action. As Ravi and Rahul entered the room where the hearing was due, they saw that the Agarwal group of lawyers was already present in full force, dressed in their power suits and looking very confident.

At dot 3 p.m., Justice Anand announced that hearing for the bail appeal of Dr Agarwal in the Rupali burn case could begin. Both the sides presented their case, with Mr Agarwal vehemently trying to burn holes in the prosecution's case. At 4 p.m. the judge put a stop to the hearing and said he would give the judgement at 4.15 p.m.

Both parties waited for the verdict, outwardly confident but nevertheless slightly anxious. At exactly 4.15 p.m., the judge reappeared and read out one line, 'The bail appeal of Dr Agarwal in the Rupali burn case is rejected and he is to be sent to judicial custody till the investigations are completed.'

Ravi and Rahul were calm but happy from within. As expected, Agarwal was absolutely livid. If it were possible, he would have manipulated the system and made the judge reverse the decision. But it was already out and they would soon receive a copy. Arvind Agarwal himself looked dejected and hung his head without saying a word. His father tried to reassure him that he would fight the case and get him out fast, but both knew it was not going to be as easy as it had seemed. Arvind would have to spend time with ordinary undertrial criminals. He was led off by the police, amidst a lot of pushing and shoving by the media trying to get a byte out of him. But he did not open his mouth; all his charm and glib talk had deserted him.

Ravi and Rahul did not say much to the media. Agarwal, however, was busy talking to them, and with his usual bluster boasted that he would get his son out soon.

That night, Ravi got a call from the inspector whom he had sent to Arvind's college campus. The information was very positive, so he decided he would have to personally handle the situation. He told the inspector to meet him at the college gate at 9 a.m. sharp the following morning.

It had occurred to Ravi that the only person who could have come at that early hour and be let in by Rupali was the milkman. There was also the evidence of spilt milk and a vessel on the floor. He had sent the inspector to find out if a milkman used to visit the Agarwals. He knew that many people still preferred fresh milk straight from a nearby dairy, rather than buying it in plastic packets. The inspector had found out that a milkman indeed supplied milk to all the doctors in C-1 building. Mrs Desai had also confirmed that on the day of Rupali's death, the milkman had come as usual. She had also revealed that his name was Roop Singh and that he had a small dairy just outside the campus. By 9 a.m. he would have finished delivering milk to all his customers and be back home.

Ravi and Jadhav, the inspector, went together to the medical college in Ravi's private car. Both were in civilian clothes.

'Sir, the dairy is behind the college campus. This road will take us right there,' explained Jadhav.

Ravi stopped his car just before the dairy and they got down. There was a motorcycle parked outside and a woman was washing milk cans with a couple of children playing around. The smell of milk and dung pervaded the air.

'Sir, it seems like a small place. I can count about ten buffaloes and six cows.'

Ravi called out, 'Is Roop Singh at home?'

'Yes,' replied the woman as she continued washing, 'he is taking a bath. Please tell me what you want.'

'We have some work with him, can we come in?'

Immediately she looked uneasy but took them into the small unpainted brick house and made them sit on a couple of metal folding chairs.

'I will go and see if he's done,' she said and went looking for her husband behind a plastic curtain that separated the tiny room from what was probably the bedroom.

Within minutes the milkman emerged, wearing his kurta as he entered. He was a huge man and heavily built. He was wearing a long thick gold chain around his neck, a silk kurta, and a coloured lungi. He also had a red and white thin cotton towel around his shoulders, a golden watch on one hand and a heavy steel kada on the other. Roop Singh was quite a personality!

He pulled out a heavy wooden stool from the inner room and sitting down asked them why they had come. Ravi knew the value of sudden shock when questioning a person like this. He told the dairy owner to send his wife out since they needed to talk alone.

The waifish wife left the room and Ravi began, 'I've been sent by Mr Rajeev Kabra.'

At once the man turned pale and looked anxious, but wiping his forehead he said that he did not know the person mentioned. Ravi took out a photo clipping from a newspaper and showed it to the milkman. 'Do you recognize him?'

Roop Singh suddenly became angry, 'Who are you, and why are you asking me about a person I do not know?'

Both Ravi and the inspector took out their identity cards and showed them to the milkman. Since Roop Singh was such a hefty man, the inspector also prominently displayed his service revolver. 'Do you want to answer our questions, or should we take you to the police chowki?'

A chastened Roop Singh sat down but repeated that he did not know the person in the picture. Ravi pushed him back against the wall. He asked the inspector to guard the man and went into the inner room.

The room was small and sparsely furnished so it did not take him long to unearth the cloth bundle of notes from a steel cupboard that was strangely kept unlocked!

'Keep guarding this man, I will come back soon,' said Ravi who had decided to question the milkman's wife.

Roop Singh's wife was sweeping the dairy and looked extremely anxious when Ravi said he'll question her after showing his credentials. He began on a soft and sympathetic note, 'I am a policeman, but do not be afraid. I want to ask you a few questions.'

'Please ask me what you want,' she answered.

'Did you know that your husband had a hand in a madam called Rupali's murder at the medical college campus?'

The milkman's wife was trembling with fear, so Ravi asked her to sit down, and again repeated the question. After a lot of cajoling she began speaking in a voice that was almost a whisper, and she broke down often, 'Sahib, I don't mind telling you that my husband is a very cruel man. He has been ill-treating and beating me all these years and it will be a relief for me if he is put in jail for a few years. I will get some peace of mind. He did not tell me anything about what he was planning, but on that day I noticed two things. One of the milk cans smelt of kerosene and his clothes also smelt of the same. He also came back earlier than he normally did and rushed in to take a bath.'

'Hmm . . . Do you know where the kerosene came from?' Ravi asked.

'Sahib we store some for use in the cooking stove when we run out of gas, but not that much. I do not know from where he procured it.'

Ravi made a mental note to check up on this. Then he asked, 'Did he have his towel draped around his shoulders when he returned?'

The woman thought for a while and then replied, 'He had worn the towel when he left, but it was missing from his clothes when I washed them.'

'Did he seem perturbed?'

'He was short-tempered with me and did not want me to ask him anything.'

'When did you come to know of the murder?'

'I had gone to the shop to buy something, when the shopkeeper told me. It did not strike me at that time, but slowly the truth dawned on me, and I was horrified. I did not dare to open my mouth in front of my husband as he would have beaten me up. Then a few days later, a car came and the driver delivered a suitcase with money in it, and my husband's mood improved after that. When I asked him who had sent the money, he said it was a loan from someone to buy our farm.

'Will you be able to manage on your own if your husband is put in jail?' Ravi asked.

'Sahib, I have absolutely no support, but will have to manage the dairy and my two children on my own. I can keep a young boy to help me deliver the milk. My elder son is twelve years old and can help me with the rest of the work. I will also sell the motorcycle so that we will have some money in our hands. And sahib, can I at least keep that money? I can buy a farm we have seen and go away from here; people will talk about my husband's arrest, and it will be difficult to continue to stay here and run the dairy.'

'I don't think that will be possible. But if anyone tries to harass you, give me a call.'

'Thank you sahib! Please do not tell my husband what I have revealed about him. I am scared that he will punish me when he comes out of jail.'

'Please do not worry. I will not reveal any of this to him.' Ravi came back to where the milkman was still being guarded by the inspector. He extracted the mobile from his kurta pocket. With the cloth bundle and mobile in his hands, he said, 'Roop Singh, I'm arresting you for the murder of Rupali Agarwal.' He then turned to the inspector, 'Handcuff him and let's quickly escort him to the car.'

Both of them walked out, pushing the burly milkman out of the house and into the back seat of the car. A small crowd of onlookers had gathered outside their dairy. Ravi now turned to the dairyman's wife who was anxiously running behind them and told her where they were taking her husband. He then got into the driver's seat and drove straight to the police headquarters to formally book Roop Singh as a suspect for the murder of Mrs Rupali Agarwal.

Once at the police station, Ravi decided to strike while the milkman was still in a state of shock. He asked Inspector Jadhav to count the money in front of Roop Singh and even as the inspector was counting, Ravi got into his storytelling mode.

'I'm going to tell you a story, Roop Singh, that'll reveal how much we already know about the part you played in Rupali's murder.' A stunned Roop Singh could only listen as Ravi began, 'On the morning of 20 August, you went as usual to flat number C-1/3 to deliver milk. Rupali madam opened the door, and after you had poured the milk, she turned around to keep the vessel in the kitchen. The routine was that she would keep the milk, come back and then close the door. On that day, you followed her, then gagged her from behind with a long red cloth towel, exactly like the one you have around your shoulders today.' Dramatically, Ravi removed the towel and told the inspector to keep it as evidence.

'You then tied her hands from behind with a thin rope and poured kerosene all over her from the second milk can that you had brought with you. After that you set her on fire and quickly left. Normally no one would have suspected you, since you came every day and apparently had no motive for killing her. But the man who had instructed you has confessed and revealed that he paid you to do it.' He turned to the inspector, 'How much is there in the bundle?'

'Fifteen lakh rupees sir.'

'Close the bundle, seal it, make a note of the amount and send the money for fingerprinting.'

Ravi turned to Roop Singh again, 'These are very big and powerful people. They will put the whole blame on you and escape themselves. If you tell the truth and accept your part, you may be let off with lesser punishment, otherwise you may even get a death sentence—the choice is yours.'

Roop Singh's massive build could not conceal his cowardly heart for long. He broke very easily and spilled the beans. He said that a man had approached him on 15 August and made a deal with him. 'He said he would pay me for a very simple job. He also told me how to do it. It was exactly as you described it. I said I would need twenty-five lakh and then we agreed on fifteen.'

'Who was this man, do you know his name?'

'No sahib, he did not tell me. He was tall, fair and was wearing dark glasses with a muffler round his neck that also covered the lower part of his face.'

Ravi took out the newspaper clipping he had showed Roop Singh before and asked him again, 'Now do you recognize him?'

Roop Singh pointed to Rajeev Kabra and said that he was probably the man who had told him to kill Rupali but he wasn't sure.

'Why are you not sure?'

'Since he was wearing dark glasses and a muffler that covered half his face, I cannot be certain, but if I hear his voice I will recognize him. It was very distinctive.'

'Distinctive? How?'

'It was harsh and rasping.'

'What about the money? Did he give you the money too?'

'No sir, the money was delivered in a suitcase by a driver on 25 August.'

'Do you remember the face of the driver and the car?'

'The car was a big white one and I will recognize the driver when I see him.'

'Was there anyone else in the car?'

'The driver had parked the car at quite a distance from my dairy but I could faintly make out that there was a man and woman in the car.'

'Okay. Tell us in your words exactly how you did it.'

Roop Singh put his head down and did not speak.

Ravi spoke firmly, 'Roop Singh, you have committed a grave crime. But if you tell the truth, you may get a lighter sentence, and I will also try to ensure that your wife and children are not rendered homeless till you come out of jail.'

The burly milkman was almost in tears. With folded hands he disclosed the story. 'Sahib, I rang the bell and as usual the doctor's wife opened the door. I poured milk into her vessel and she turned back towards the kitchen. I jumped at her and used my towel to gag her. The vessel fell from her hands and there was a noise. But luckily it fell on the mat and the noise was more like a thud. For a moment I was scared that doctor sahib would have heard the sound and would come running out, but nothing happened.

'I quickly tied her hands behind her back with a thin rope. Then I poured kerosene on her, struck a matchstick and set her on fire. I then walked away quietly. Since I had rehearsed these actions in my mind a number of times, I did not feel anything while performing the deed. It was only afterwards that the enormity of what I had done sank in.'

'Why did you leave the door open?'

'Those were the instructions given to me.'

Roop Singh had reached a state of catharsis, in which he hardly realized, or did not care how much he was implicating himself. He put his head down again and paused for some more time.

Ravi left him alone for a minute then asked him if his wife knew what he had done. 'Yes, I think she knows. When I got home, I changed my clothes and asked her to wash out the cans. She pointedly asked me why I had not delivered all the milk that day. I told her not to ask me any questions. She washed out the cans and later in the day came to know of the death in the campus. She came back and told me about it. Her suspicions were aroused since one of the cans had smelt of kerosene, and she eyed me uneasily throughout the day. A few days later, the suitcase full of money that was delivered to me must have confirmed her suspicions.'

'Where is the suitcase?'

'I removed the money from it, bundled up the notes in a big sheet and put them in the cupboard where you found them. The empty suitcase is still in the loft. My wife wanted to know why I had received such a lot of money, but I lied to her that it was a loan.

'Recently, the corporation people have been harassing me to shift my dairy out of the city premises as it has become a health hazard. I wanted to buy a farm that I had seen outside the city, and when this person came with his proposal and said he would offer me a lot of money, I could only think of my farm. I immediately said I would need twenty-five lakh. He agreed to give me fifteen. I do not own the land I run my dairy in, sahib. I had illegally occupied it about ten years back. So if I shift from here, I will not get any compensation. In fact, I was to complete the deal of the farm today. The man is expected in about an hour's time. If you had come tomorrow we would not have been here since I would have shifted.'

Roop Singh stopped talking and Ravi made him sign the statement after reading it. The milkman went through it painstakingly before affixing his signature at the bottom.

'Sahib, because of my desperation I agreed to do the job, but that madam's face haunts me every moment.'

'Roop Singh, you may be let off with a lighter sentence because you have cooperated with us,' Ravi's voice was soft as he could sense that the dairyman was remorseful. He turned to the inspector and said, 'I want you to keep what you have heard a secret. If there is a leak I'll know you are responsible. I like the way you work and think you have a bright future, don't give it all away.'

Jadhav saluted smartly and replied, 'Sir, I would never let you down. I respect you a lot.'

Ravi made a mental note that they must have the empty suitcase picked up from Roop Singh's house. He met Rahul that evening and brought him up to date. His junior was jubilant at the breakthrough.

'Chief, is it possible that Arvind Agarwal heard nothing?'

'Rahul, it is possible that he had had a couple of drinks and watched TV late into the night. He would have probably been sleeping so soundly that the noise of the vessel falling did not penetrate his consciousness. Also, the vessel was full, so it would not make such a loud sound, and Roop Singh says it fell on the mat, further dulling its impact. But later some sound from Rupali must have reached him, since he was trying to smother Rupali's flames.'

'Should we release him now?'

'No, let him cool his heels for a few more days. It will do him good.'

Ravi and Rahul also decided that the next few days they would concentrate on the S.N. Rao murder case. They now had enough ammunition to tackle the big guns in the cricket board.

Fourteen

'Rahul, let's review all the cases,' Ravi said. They had fixed up this day to go through all the leads they had got on the different cases up to now.

'Look here:

'Mane's death–August 11;

'Rupali's death–August 20;

'Sunanda's death–August 30;

'S.N. Rao's death–September 10.

'Rupali was giving tuitions to Rajeev Kabra's daughter at his residence, and Sunanda was having an affair with Kabra. There has to be a common thread to the murders when we see a pattern like this emerging. The four deaths are clearly connected to the cricket board in some way. Now I see why Ajay wanted us to investigate the Rupali and Sunanda cases too. All the reporters of his channel have been ferreting out cases connected even remotely to the cricket board. When Ramesh Patel saw that there could be a connection with the board in Sunanda's and Rupali's murders, he got us into the act.'

'Yes, that seems to be the case,' Rahul answered.

'The most difficult part in solving these cases has now begun for us,' said Ravi, 'that of questioning the big fish in the cricket board. We have quite a bit of evidence against

Rajeev Kabra, and his co-conspirator was probably Hansraj Verma, as they are said to be very close. Were any of the others involved? Should we question everyone or only the main players?'

After a lot of consideration, Ravi rang up the board and asked the secretary to call up Manik Jindal, Hansraj Verma and Rajeev Kabra and request them to be present at 9 a.m. the next day in the office. He told him that it was for a routine questioning session in the Rao murder case.

In the meantime he decided to read about their background, sourced and rewritten by Rahul from the dossiers he had obtained from the intelligence department. He began with Manik Jindal:

> Born to a lawyer couple, Manik has a younger brother who has taken up their parents' profession. But Manik himself did not want to be a lawyer. He had always been a brilliant student and also represented his school and college, and then Delhi state in cricket. He was an opening batsman and for some time, had ambitions of becoming a professional cricketer, but he also wanted to be a doctor. He therefore studied medicine and specialized in orthopaedics, but continued to play for Delhi whenever he could.
>
> It was when Manik became president of the Indian Medical Association that he came in contact with local politicians. It was not surprising then that Jindal was soon approached by a political party to join them. At first he was reluctant to do so, since he was not inclined towards politics. But under sustained pressure, he gave in and became one of the leading lights of his party within a decade.
>
> Manik had helped Hansraj Verma with some orthopaedic problems and become his friend, especially

since he was also the head of Delhi Cricket Association by then. So when Hansraj Verma asked him if he would like to become a member of the national board, Manik jumped at the idea. True to his word, his mentor got Manik elected into the board within a few months.

Recently, Manik has added another feather to his cap by becoming chairman of ITL.

They next read the report on Hansraj Verma and learnt that when Verma was fifty, he became head of the cricket board of his state, Rajasthan, and within a few years, using his money, clout and political connections, got himself elected to the national board. Rajeev Kabra's dossier revealed that he meticulously maintained a diary, with names, professions, phone numbers and addresses of all those he had helped or befriended. And he never hesitated in utilizing these contacts when he needed them. After becoming the head of his state's cricket board, he was noticed by Hansraj Verma, who helped him get elected to the national board.

After going through all the information, Ravi said, 'Let me summarize the case so far so that we'll have the facts fresh in our minds when we tackle the board members. The facts regarding S.N. Rao's death are that there was a secret group within the board. This group was unhappy with Rao for voicing his dissent regarding the treatment given to TLI and to Mane.

'Besides Rajeev Kabra who else can we think belonged to this group? Probably Manik Jindal and Hansraj Verma. They also felt threatened by Rao because of his holier-than-thou attitude and because he possessed inside knowledge of their siphoning off money for funding a major opposition party. Meanwhile Mane, the former treasurer, was repeatedly trying to resurface. He had to be eased out since he could prove a very serious threat to their power base in the board.

'We know that after Mane's death, Rajeev Kabra had wanted to send a congratulatory mail to one of the board members, probably Hansraj Verma, but accidentally ended up clicking on Rao's mail ID. This increased the group's paranoid threat perception from Rao.

'Meanwhile, Rajeev Kabra approached Arora of Ace Detective Agency to provide a full dossier on Rao including details of his itinerary for the following month. We know that this dossier also gave them the interesting and important information about Vineet's strained relationship with his father and their planned visit to the farmhouse. They decided to meet Vineet with the plan to eliminate his father and offered huge incentives including clearing all his debts and membership of the board in his father's place. Vineet probably saw this as a solution to all his problems and fell in line.' Ravi looked up at Rahul.

Rahul nodded, 'So far it makes perfect sense sir.'

'Yes . . . everything seems to be falling in place, doesn't it? Now let's look at Mane's death. It was also a murder as far as we can see. Rajeev Kabra's incriminating mail in Rao's inbox and Vijay Kumar's confession that he was used by Rajeev Kabra all prove that. Do you think Manik Jindal or Hansraj Verma played a role in it?'

Rahul replied, 'There is a strong possibility. But shouldn't we also look at the Rupali murder case to see where it fits in?'

'Yes, of course.' Ravi went back to his analyses according to the data they had collected, 'Rupali was giving tuitions in Rajeev Kabra's house. One day she overheard Kabra and, possibly, Verma plotting the murder of S.N. Rao. What she heard was too damaging for them to let her live. Here, Roop Singh was recruited to murder Rupali. What about Arvind Agarwal? Did he have a hand in his wife's murder?

'Rahul, periodically summarizing the case in this fashion helps in refreshing the main facts in our minds and discovering loopholes in our investigation. I now know how I'll tackle the big guns tomorrow. Let's get a good night's sleep tonight. We'll need all our physical and mental faculties about us when we question them. But before that, let's see what information we can gather about the Indian cricket board and its finances from the internet.'

'Chief, I've already done that. I have collected some facts, but if we want more, I can get it by going to their website,' Rahul said, handing over the printouts of the information he had collected.

'Good work Rahul, I'll read all this in the night. I hope you have gone through it once.'

'Yes I have, chief!' beamed Rahul. 'I have a copy of this too.'

∼

That night, in the comfort of his home, Ravi read the printouts Rahul had given him. He was sure the clue to the string of recent murders lay somewhere in these details. He discovered that the financial stakes in the leagues were very high—high enough to provide the motive for the murders. A group of power brokers is probably operating from inside the board that will go to any lengths to retain control over the board's finances, he concluded. Things were beginning to look murkier.

∼

The next morning Ravi and Rahul reached the Delhi cricket board office sharp at nine. This was a rare occasion when they would be questioning so many big guns in one sitting.

A small office had been set aside for the session, and both of them settled in to wait for the three people they were to question. As Rahul marvelled at the opulence of the office itself, Ravi decided that they would begin with whoever came in first.

The first person to walk in was Manik Jindal who came in at 9.30 a.m. Ravi wished him, shook hands and pointedly looked at his watch.

'Sir, without wasting time, I'm going to begin. As you know, we are investigating the sports minister, S.N. Rao's death and in that context, we have come to ask you a few routine questions.' Rahul sat quietly with his notepad ready to write details of what was to be discussed and some that was only to be deduced!

Besides being a doctor, Manik was one of the shrewdest politicians around, and was not going to give away anything easily. He nodded politely. 'Please go ahead. I'll answer to the best of my ability,' he said, waving his hand. Rahul noted the branded watch Manik wore.

'What do you know about S.N. Rao's death?'

'Only what I've read in the newspapers and seen on television.'

'Did you have any prior knowledge of his death?'

'No.' He was answering very comfortably.

'Tell me sir, how were your relations with your deceased colleague?'

'He was a good friend. I got along very well with him,' Manik answered.

'Were there any disagreements between you two?' Ravi asked and even before Manik answered he knew the clichéd response he would get.

'Disagreements are always there among friends, but they are discussed and sorted out.'

'Were there any disagreements that could not be sorted out?'

'No.' Manik seemed to be hell-bent on divulging nothing.

Ravi probed further and even though he knew he would not get any answers, he waited for bodily signs, 'Did you meet his son Vineet?'

'I have met him at functions,' was Manik's casual response.

'When was the last time you met him?'

'During the T20 matches.'

'Did you not meet him after that?'

'No. There was no need to.'

'Did you have any discussion about Vineet with other members of the board?'

'No.'

'Did you have any discussion about S.N. Rao with other members of the board?' Ravi asked casually.

'Yes, we discussed the fact that he did not like "how Mane had been treated" but this was an internal tactical discussion and had nothing to do with Rao's death.'

'Were any decisions taken in these meetings to ease out Rao from the board?'

'I don't think that is of any relevance here.'

Ravi knew this was a critical question, but he let it go. He did not want the people behind the murders to be alarmed.

'Is there anything that you'd like to discuss with us? Any information that could prove useful in solving this case?'

'I don't think so,' Manik replied.

Ravi rose up and so did Rahul and Manik. 'Well I think that will be all Dr Jindal, thank you for your cooperation. We may get back to you later, and do call us if you have any information that may be relevant to the case. We would like to request you to sit in the next room till we have finished our sessions with the others.'

Manik nodded and walked briskly out of the room.

He was followed by the suave Rajeev Kabra who walked in arrogantly, revealing that he was more than confident of his status and power. Ravi knew he was a slippery customer but had enough experience to handle people like him. Once the balloon was deflated, such people became soft and easy to manage.

Ravi decided to do his storytelling act and began, 'Good morning Mr Kabra, please sit down. You know we are here to find out what knowledge you have of the sports minister's death. Let me first tell you a few things that we do know, and then you can add to our knowledge.'

Ravi had decided that he would not put all his cards on the table but reveal only enough to scare Rajeev Kabra. He went on to first talk about what they knew about Kabra's background. He then paused and said that the next bit might come as a surprise.

'A reporter from a TV channel saw the exchange between you and the owner of Ace Detective Agency in front of Kay-Pee mall on the evening of 16 August. Since he recognized you, he felt the meeting maybe newsworthy. He therefore followed Mr Arora and saw that he owned a detective agency. He spoke to his boss about the encounter, and they decided to keep quiet for some time. But later the news of S.N. Rao's death broke and Vineet was arrested, as foul play was suspected.

'Then there were rumours that the cricket board may be involved and the reporter thought that the meeting he had witnessed might in some way be connected to the murder. He decided to meet the proprietor of the detective agency. He went to the agency and asked Mr Arora specifically about what was exchanged that day, and the latter under threat of police action handed over material that was extremely explosive.'

Ravi paused to build up the suspense and then asked, 'What do you think were its contents Mr Kabra?'

Rajeev Kabra's smile remained intact, 'I really do not know; you are the one telling the story, you tell me.'

'I thought you would complete the story, but never mind, I'll do it for you Mr Kabra. The contents revealed that you had commissioned the detective to investigate the background of the new board members.'

Rajeev Kabra breathed an inner sigh of relief. *So the idiot Arora had enough sense not to reveal anything about the big job and had warded off the reporter with innocuous material.*

Ravi knew exactly what Rajeev Kabra was thinking. 'I am nearing the end of my story now, Mr Kabra. This reporter that we are talking about, approached us saying he was not satisfied by the detective's response and was certain that the material exchanged pertained to the present case. We then visited Mr Arora and using our persuasive powers managed to get the real material that was exchanged on that day. Now do you have anything to say?'

Rajeev Kabra remained sullenly silent, so Ravi went for the kill, 'You Mr Kabra, in your individual capacity, or on behalf of some other members of the cricket board, commissioned Arora to prepare a dossier on S.N. Rao that included his appointments and proposed activities for a month. And knowing he had planned a weekend visit with his son to the farmhouse, you roped in Vineet to implement your plan of eliminating Rao. We know that Vineet was inducted into the plan and exactly how it was carried out. As to the motive, we know that too. Rao was a businessman and to that extent was happy at the way the board's fortunes were skyrocketing, but he was not very happy with some of the *methods* being employed to gain these ends. And he was especially unhappy about how you guys had treated Mane and the TLI. And also about how a big percentage of the incoming money that was unaccounted for, was being siphoned off to fund a major political party.

'Slowly you were realizing that he could prove to be an impediment to your extremely ambitious future plans to make the Indian cricket board and the people running it, the richest and most powerful in the world. Rao was proving a moral block for you and he had too much inside knowledge of your "working" methods. So you decided that he would have to be removed from the picture. Which of the other members were involved with you we do not know but will find out pretty soon.'

Rajeev Kabra stood up angrily, 'DCP Sharma, you are making extremely serious allegations and I will not respond without consulting my lawyer.'

'Please do so, because you are going to need him. I am actually not done yet; I have evidence of your involvement in three other cases, but maybe we can continue this session later in front of your lawyer. Now can you please wait in the next room along with Mr Manik Jindal, till we have finished our session with Mr Verma?'

Rajeev Kabra was furious as he walked out with his mobile, obviously about to call his lawyer.

The last to walk in was the automobile tycoon, Hansraj Verma. Ravi had a lot of regard for this gritty and hard-working industrialist.

'Sir,' he began, 'this is a routine questioning session regarding S.N. Rao's death.'

'Please go ahead, I will cooperate with you,' Hansraj responded.

'Before I ask any questions, let me tell you about what we know already.'

'Okay.'

Ravi first repeated what he had told Rajeev Kabra regarding the evidence they had of the board's involvement in Rao's murder. Then he paused before resuming, 'I also want to talk about an incident that occurred some time back in Rajeev Kabra's house that has a direct bearing on another murder case.'

A crease had developed on Verma's forehead, but he did not react.

'Rajeev Kabra's daughter was taking tuitions from a physics lecturer at his house, and sometime back this teacher was removed from her assignment.' Ravi paused again before continuing, 'Can you tell me why she was fired?'

'I suppose his daughter must have found her to be incompetent, so he would have asked her to leave. In any case, why are you asking *me* this question?'

'You will soon understand. Could there have been any other reason for her being fired?'

'DCP Sharma, what are you driving at? Why don't you come straight to the point?' Hansraj seemed to be losing his temper.

'Fine. We know that she was fired because she had overheard a highly incriminating conversation between you and Rajeev Kabra.'

Hansraj's eyes narrowed, 'And what was this conversation about, since you seem to know all that happens behind closed doors?'

'You two were discussing various methods by which Rao could be gotten rid off.'

'By "rid off" you mean?'

'We have reason to believe that you were planning to eliminate him permanently.'

'What rubbish!'

'We have strong proof of this.'

Hansraj gave out an exasperated sigh, 'Well this has gone far enough, and I will not speak a word more without consulting my lawyer.'

'As you please sir.'

'Good day DCP!' Verma walked out.

Ravi turned to his colleague, 'Rahul, this is not going to be easy; not that I expected otherwise. These are high-level wheeler-dealers who will try hard to throw us off the track. Our job will be to somehow stick on and take things to their conclusion.

'I am sure we have stirred up a hornet's nest and can expect some action soon. You can ask the board members to leave now, and let us also do so.'

Rahul was perturbed, 'But chief, today's session seems half-finished. We haven't brought things to a satisfactory conclusion!'

'These are very big people we are dealing with, Rahul. We have pricked them where it hurts, now it's their turn to react. From hereon we play a game of chess where both parties make moves and countermoves till the game ends. We can only hope we emerge on the winning side. Come on, let's leave!'

For the first time, Rahul was dissatisfied with Ravi's handling of the situation. Was his senior overawed by the sheer persona of the board members? Or was he purposely going slow? Why had he shown lack of courage today? It was so unlike him . . .

Outside, the media had collected in hordes to find out what was going on—there was the usual click of cameras, journalists shouting out their questions, mikes being thrust in the policemen's faces. But Ravi, in his usual style, said that they would be holding a press conference later. Then he quickly got into the police jeep with Rahul and sped away.

Fifteen

As soon as they reached the police headquarters, Ravi entered his room followed by Rahul. Even before he reached his desk, the phone rang. It was Director General Khanna, asking him to immediately come to his office. *So, the board members had not wasted any time!*

He smiled wryly at Rahul and told him whose call it was. But before leaving he asked his junior to remove whatever information he could from Rao's file and also delete the same material from the soft copy in his computer. 'We anyway have a copy on my home computer and can take another printout if needed,' he said. 'Especially remove all the papers to do with the other three cases, since I am sure they will take away the case from us and I don't want to give away our hard-earned information to anyone. First work on the paper file, we will give them the soft copy only if they ask for it.'

'I understand chief and will get going immediately. Don't worry, I know what to do!'

Ravi then hurriedly left for the DGP's office. As he entered he saw that the commissioner was also there. DGP Khanna asked him to shut the door and sit down.

'Ravi, what the hell is happening! You went to question a person of Hansraj Verma's stature and didn't keep us informed?' the DGP demanded.

'Sir, it was only a routine questioning session, and as soon as I would have got something concrete, I would have updated you both,' Ravi answered, trying to placate his boss.

His words fell on deaf ears. 'But, according to what Hansraj Verma tells me, your questioning was anything but "routine". He said you made all sorts of allegations.'

'Sir, the allegations were based on certain leads we had received, and I employed standard methods of questioning.'

'Please hand over the file to me, I'll go through it and will decide what to do next. Till then, I request you not to talk to anyone about this case. It is just too big for you to handle on your own!'

The commissioner remained silent. Ravi saluted and left the room promising to return with the file.

By the time he reached his room, he was seething with anger. His reputation was such that however unconventional his approach to solving a case, his seniors had always stood by him and treated him with respect. But DGP Khanna was new and was said to have high-level political connections.

'Rahul, it has happened, they will most probably take the case away from us. I have an inkling that they will derail everything and make sure that the main players are let off scot-free. They are asking for the file, have you done what I had asked you to do?'

'Yes chief, I had enough time to do what you wanted. Here's the file with as little information as we can possibly give them.' Rahul handed over the file to his senior.

A wicked smile spread across Ravi's face, 'Good work Rahul! I'll hand this over to them and let's see what happens.'

Then Ravi rushed back to the DGP's office with the abridged version of the file and gave it to him.

DGP Khanna seemed pleased, 'Thank you Ravi for the prompt response. I'll go through it and call you.'

Rahul meanwhile copied out all the relevant data from Ravi's PC on to two pen drives and left behind the same amount of information that they had handed over to the DGP in the files. As soon as Ravi returned, Rahul showed him what he had done.

'Great work junior, I know I can always depend on you!'

Rahul and Ravi decided to meet at the latter's house after office hours. They had a habit of going full throttle at cases that they took up, without resting till these were solved. So it was disheartening to be stopped suddenly in their tracks. They carried on with their routine work till 5 p.m., and then Ravi called the DGP to check with him as to what he was supposed to do.

DGP Khanna was polite but firm, 'Ravi, it is a highly sensitive case involving very important people, and could have political ramifications, so I can answer your query only after consulting the home ministry. I will let you know after meeting with them. Tomorrow is Saturday, call me on Monday, and I'll let you know then if you can continue with the case.' Ravi had to be satisfied with that. He felt as though he would burst with anger. The only comforting thought was that they had not disclosed everything.

Both of them left for Ravi's home at 6 p.m. to decide on further course of action. Once inside the house, Ravi ordered dinner from a catering service and Rahul rang up his home to tell them he would eat with his boss and return late. Even as they were waiting for the food to arrive, Ravi turned to Rahul, 'What happened to the transcription from the mobiles? We had the mobiles of Rao, Vineet, the security guard and caretaker at the farmhouse. We have also given the mobiles of Sunanda, Neela and Arvind Agarwal to them. Find out if they've completed the job yet. If it is ready, I want the reports now. We are not off the case till we are officially told so.' Rahul made a note of this.

Ravi gave further instructions, 'Secondly, what about the forensic report of the various containers we had collected from the farmhouse, and the one from Mane's house? Check on that too. Try to get all these pieces of evidence. If we get a positive feedback from these two sources, we can move in for the kill. And before I forget, also check if the handwriting expert has given his report on the analysis of the writing on the wall of the farmhouse, and whether the computer guys were able to get anything from Arvind's PC.'

Rahul got down to work immediately. He rang up both the numbers and found out that the phone transcription and chemical analysis reports were ready. He asked them to deliver the reports immediately to Ravi's house. The handwriting expert also said he would call back and, if possible, send in his report. The computer experts reported that they had not found anything incriminating in Arvind's PC.

'Now,' Ravi began, pulling out a bottle of whisky, 'suppose they take away the case from us, as I think they will, then I have a plan. We move full steam ahead to a stage where it will be difficult for them to sweep things under the carpet. Another thing we could do is to hand over all the incriminating material we have to Ajay Shukla. Then we can get Ex-el channel to make a lot of noise and take all the credit for "solving" the case, even as we do all the work behind the scenes. One thing I've decided is that I'll not give up, whatever may happen. In our country, the big fish always get away so someone has to bring a few of them to book. Once the message goes out that all are equal under the law of the land, it will be easier the next time around.' Rahul went and brought two glasses and an ice-tray from the kitchen. They were in the living room of Ravi's sparsely furnished bachelor pad.

'Media has a big role to play in this,' Ravi continued, 'If they make enough noise, it will be difficult to stop these guys from being prosecuted, so we shall use them.'

Suddenly the door bell rang. 'I think that's our dinner. Let's have the food before we go on.' For a few moments they were involved in serving themselves food from the packets. Then they settled down with the drinks to a comfortable discussion.

'Chief, I've never seen you so upset,' Rahul spoke with a mouthful. 'I really hope we get to complete the case. Also, I want to make a confession. Today after coming out from the cricket board office, I had my reservations about the way you had handled things. I thought you were being soft with them. But I now realize that you knew what you were doing all along and I am ashamed of having doubted you.'

'Don't worry Rahul, I'll find a way around this situation. Regarding my handling of the board members, I had to do a balancing act by placing some of my cards on the table, without revealing them all. I knew you were not happy, but don't worry, eventually we will succeed.'

They ate in silence trying to work the problem in their minds. Just as they had settled in their seats after dinner, the doorbell rang again and a police constable saluted and delivered a packet. It contained the detailed report on the SMSes received, beginning from a month before to date, in all the mobile phones they had sent for transcription. Rahul and Ravi split the reports between them. They first identified the numbers they recognized and ticked them, and then tried to find out the identity of the ones they did not recognize.

Vineet had received many calls from Rajeev Kabra. He had also received a message asking 'Health ok?' that could possibly mean that he was asking whether he was going along with the plan.

The security guard had made and received many calls. There seemed to be one number from which he had received maximum calls, but that number was unfamiliar. Ravi contacted the people who had sent in the transcriptions and told them he needed them to trace the identity of that number. He got a call in fifteen minutes that the number belonged to Rajeev Kabra's wife, Damini Kabra. Ravi got excited; this could only mean that Rajeev Kabra was in touch with both the security guard and Vineet. In all probability, he had used his wife's mobile to call and send messages to the guard. Rajeev Kabra could get away by defending the SMS messages sent to Vineet. He could say they pertained to the health of Vineet's father or even his own. But there was no way he could explain away the ones made to S.N. Rao's security guard!

Sunanda's phone revealed that she had received many SMSes from both Sanjay and Rajeev Kabra. She seemed to have been meeting both of them outside the house. Since Sanjay had got married to Neela, Sunanda had probably revived her contact with Rajeev Kabra. So, they now had concrete evidence that Rajeev Kabra had been in constant touch with Sunanda.

Meanwhile, the chemical analysis reports of the containers also arrived.

There had been five containers that Ravi and the inspector had labelled, sealed and sent for chemical analysis. They were numbered I, II, III, IV and V.

No. I was the one they'd found outside Vineet's bathroom window, and the analysis showed it contained some kind of tobacco paste.

No. II was the dispensing bottle found in the corner of the lawn, and it had contained a cough formula.

No. III was the bottle with a dropper found partially

buried under the bougainvillea tree, and it had contained some eye drops.

No. IV was the container found buried deep in the overgrown grass in the gutter outside the farmhouse. This showed traces of tincture aconitine.

No. V was the container found in Mane's house. This also showed evidence of the same poison, tincture aconitine.

'Rahul, here it is, direct evidence of poison found from the venues of the murders. Rajeev Kabra had inducted both Vineet and the security guard into the plan. I'm sure neither of them knew that the other person was also involved. The plan was to put the required dose of the poison into the paans that would be served to Rao. Immediately after eating them, he would retire for the night. Vineet would take away his mobile and lock the door from outside. Rao would struggle alone in his room and because of the air conditioner and fortunately for them, the thundershowers, his calls for help went unheard. He could also not phone or rush out to find help. After six hours Vineet, as per instructions, went back, opened the door, replaced the mobile and came out.

'Both Vineet and the security guard could have laced the paans with the tincture. Both could have locked the door from outside and reopened it later. But removing the mobile and replacing it again, although easy for Vineet, was a risky proposition for the security guard.

'The latter's role was probably restricted to procuring and adding poison to the paans. He seemed to have received fifty thousand as an advance for his services. Perhaps the major part of the agreed amount would have been paid later. Rajeev Kabra must have felt that it would be too much to expect or a risk for Vineet to add the poison. He was probably also kept in the dark as to the exact method of murder. He must have been told that the plain paans were for him and the sweet ones for his father. The plan could have gone wrong if Vineet had wanted to eat sweet paan that day. But Rajeev Kabra probably knew that Vineet never ate sweet paan. It also seems he knew everything about aconite poisoning. Maybe he learnt it from the person who supplied it to them, or read about it on the net; or did Dr Jindal tell them about it?' The two policemen made a note that they should find out. Ravi continued, 'Mane's murder was simpler since only Vijay Kumar was involved—'

Just then Rahul received a call from the handwriting expert that made him happy.

'Chief, he says that there is a 90 per cent match to that of S.N. Rao's. He will send the written report tomorrow.'

'Great!' Ravi said, slapping his hand on the table. 'Now, the logical step would be to arrest Rajeev Kabra and later maybe Hansraj Verma if we are able to gather some evidence against him. I do not think the others were involved, at least not directly; otherwise we would have got something on them by now.' Then he suddenly asked, 'Rahul, do you have a bank locker?'

His junior smiled, 'What would I do with one, chief, I don't have either jewellery or black money, but my mother has one in the National Bank.'

'Tell your mother that you want to keep some important documents in her locker. We'll get all these documents photocopied. I will keep one copy and the other set I want you to keep in her locker first thing tomorrow along with one storage device with the soft copy you made. If they don't let us proceed with the case, as is likely, I think I'll hand over everything to Ajay Shukla and let Ex-el channel carry out an exposé.

'However, if we are lucky, and are allowed to carry on, we'll arrest Rajeev Kabra on Monday itself. We have more than enough evidence against him. But one more task remains. We have to try to unearth the person who sold the poison to Kabra. Dr Gupta told us that aconite was a commonly used poison and easily procured in rural areas where it is used for killing cattle, and sometimes for committing murder. I have a hunch that the poison came from Rajeev Kabra's village. Tomorrow is Sunday, let's leave early and drive down there and see what we can find. We can return by night.'

The next day, Ravi and Rahul drove down to Rajeev Kabra's village in plain clothes. They enquired around for a medicine to kill cattle, and they were told that there was only one man who supplied the kind of stuff they wanted. He ran a mutton shop on the outskirts of the village. They found the man quite easily and he agreed to sell them the poison without asking what it was for. He said he would charge a thousand rupees, and within minutes came out with the aconite tincture. There were also printed instructions on how to use it, and the way it acted!

Ravi was delighted to see that the container was similar to the one that had been found at Rao's farmhouse and in Mane's house. He turned to the man, 'We have been sent by Mr Rajeev Kabra and he said that you would give us a good rate.' Then he gave him a description of what Kabra looked like.

The man's face suddenly grew animated. 'Arre! You should have told me before that big sahib had sent you. We are very proud of him in this village and he has promised to do a lot for us. Since he has sent you, I will charge only Rs 500.'

When Ravi prodded him further he revealed that Rajeev Kabra had visited him twice during the rainy season.

On Monday morning, as expected, Ravi was summoned to the DGP's office and told that the home ministry had decided that the issue was far too big for an officer of his level to handle and the matter would be handed over to the Central Bureau of Investigation. DGP Khanna requested him to take it in the right spirit and to cooperate with the CBI in solving the case. Ravi told him that he would do whatever was required of him and came away. He knew that he carried a few aces since they had kept most of the investigation details with themselves. He was glad that the CP had trusted him enough not to probe too deeply till the case was solved.

Ravi now called Ajay Shukla and told him to meet him for lunch at a well-known dhaba outside the city. He told Rahul to cover up for him with whatever excuse he could, till he got back. Since it was a long drive to the dhaba, he started off immediately. In his jeep were copies of all the classified documents that they had.

Outside, he didn't have to duck the media. He stopped, smiled wryly at them, and leisurely announced, 'I'm no longer in charge of the case. It's now in the hands of the CBI. Henceforth you guys can look to them for bytes, and hopefully you will get a less reticent person than me as a spokesperson!'

There was a roar of laughter as Ravi quickly got into his jeep and left.

In a little more than an hour he was near the eatery. He parked his vehicle at a small distance from the roadside restaurant, changed into a plain shirt and walked in. Ajay Shukla had already reached and was sitting at a wooden table away from the crowd. He eagerly came forward to greet Ravi. When they were seated, they ordered tea and told the waiter that they would call for lunch later.

As soon as the tea came, Ravi started talking, 'First of all, let me thank you for all the leads given by you, they've been extremely useful. You must have heard that the CBI has taken over and the case is now out of my hands. But I don't want the big guns to go scot-free. I want to make a deal with Ex-el TV . . .' He paused.

Ajay looked excited. He urged Ravi, 'Go on . . .'

'I promised you breaking news but I am going to go much beyond that. I want nothing from you in return, except to broadcast what I tell you, without revealing your source. I'll give you one bit of major news every few days and I am sure you will make a lot of noise since your targets are the same as mine.'

'We will be happy to cooperate but I need to consult with Mr Patel.'

'Please call him and I'll speak to him.'

Ajay immediately sent an SMS on the private mobile number that the television magnate had given him. Within a minute there was a call back from Patel on Shukla's phone. Ravi quickly introduced himself and gave him the background. Patel said he was absolutely delighted at the prospect of receiving such sensational material on a platter, and promised Ravi that secrecy would be maintained as to the source from his channel's side.

Ravi then turned to the reporter, 'Ajay, the first step is to broadcast the news that aconite was the poison used to kill S.N. Rao. Here's a printout that tells you everything about it.'

Both then quickly ordered and had lunch before Ajay rushed off to broadcast the news the same afternoon, quoting 'reliable' sources. There was an immediate pandemonium as other channels also picked up the news and there were endless speculations. The CBI officers were left-red faced as they could neither corroborate nor negate the news. After that there was 'breaking news' every few days, and so much noise was generated by the print and electronic media that it was difficult for the CBI to sweep things under the carpet.

The home ministry came under fire, as did the government. There were calls for resignation of the home minister by the Opposition, if results were not shown fast. The media wanted to know how a TV channel could do better investigative work than the premier investigative agency of the nation.

The CBI approached Ex-el news channel, but they refused to reveal their sources. Finally, they had to turn back to Ravi for his 'cooperation'. The CBI chief and DGP Khanna summoned him to a meeting.

'Ravi,' said the DGP, 'you are the only one with enough talent and perseverance to get results fast. We want you to spearhead the case again.'

'Sir, I'd be happy to do so, but there should be no more interference from any quarter,' Ravi said, his face deadpan, even though he was delighted from inside.

'Ravi, you know the home ministry is personally interested in this case and we will have to keep them informed at every step. We want you to give us a daily report and we will decide what action to take.'

'With due respect sir, I don't work that way. I like to move very fast and take split-second decisions. In a criminal investigation, justice delayed is certainly justice denied. I am willing to give a weekly report to the CBI, but want a free hand in my work to deliver positive results.'

Ravi was deliberately not willing to read between the lines of what the DGP was trying to convey to him—*investigate, but do not take the case to its logical conclusion*. And he also knew that he would have been transferred by now if it were not for the Prime Minister, who had been a close friend of

Rao's and would not have kept quiet had he felt that the investigation was being derailed.

'Sir, I want only my ACP to work with me. If I need any help I will ask you, but like I said before, I want a free hand.' He looked stubbornly at his superior. They had to reluctantly agree to his terms.

Ravi left the office with a smile. He knew he would nail the culprits now!

Sixteen

Next day itself, Ravi prepared a case against Rajeev Kabra. He secured an arrest warrant on that basis and armed with it, arrested him. They still did not have enough evidence against Hansraj Verma or any of the others. The first to announce this 'breaking news' was obviously Ex-el channel. The hue and cry was now unimaginable, as everyone expected more arrests. Any scandal to do with the cricket board was enough to ensure the highest TRP ratings and all channels tried to outdo each other in their reporting. They carried mainly this news the whole day and speculations were rife as to the fate of the other members of the board. Anyone remotely connected to cricket or politics had become an 'expert' on the topic. There were innumerable talk shows, SMS polls, and panel discussions to do with the case—all good fodder for twenty-four-hour news channels.

Ravi had the three arrested individuals, Rajeev Kabra, the security guard and Vineet, subjected to everything from a polygraph test, the lie detector test, to brain mapping, and psychoanalysis. No conclusive results could be reached at the end of the tests conducted on Rajeev Kabra and Vineet. The security guard, however, cracked while undergoing the polygraph test. Ravi was present during the session and told Dr Dixit, the expert conducting the test, what questions to ask.

The Premier Murder League

He knew that the polygraph machine continuously records the examinee's blood pressure, heart rate, respiratory rate and body movements in the form of graphs. By reading these graphs experts are able to deduce whether the person being questioned is telling the truth or not.

'The results are not admissible in court as you very well know. However, using the information that we gather, you can put pressure on him to give a statement. Would you like me to go on?' she asked, one pointed eyebrow going up.

'Yes of course, please go on,' Ravi replied eagerly.

Dr Dixit started asking questions, interspersing innocuous ones with those that were relevant, 'Is your name Balram Singh?'

The security guard replied in a slow but clear voice, 'Yes.'

'Do you have two children?'

'Yes.'

'Were you at the farmhouse on 10 September?'

'Yes.'

Ravi was following the responses carefully.

'Did you put poison in the paans that you gave to your sahibs?'

There was silence.

The doctor then asked, 'Is your younger son's name Sonu?'

'Yes.'

'Did you put a liquid from a bottle into the paans you had bought that night?'

'Yes.' Dr Dixit gave a triumphant glance to Ravi.

She continued, 'Do you live in Delhi?'

'Yes.'

'Did you know that the liquid was poison?'

'No.'

But the polygraph revealed that the security man was lying.

The session went on in this way. It was an extremely tedious and slow procedure, but at the end of it they managed to piece together a confession.

Balram Singh admitted to being approached by a man whose name he did not know, but the description fitted Rajeev Kabra's physical description. He was told that when S.N. Rao came to the farmhouse, he had to bring four extra-large paans and give them to Vineet. Two would be sweet, for Rao, and the other two plain ones for Vineet. Before handing them over, he had to add a few drops of the liquid provided to him to Rao's paans. The procedure was simple: unfold the paans, add the liquid and seal them again with cloves.

Balram Singh had used two cloves and coconut gratings to identify the sweet paans. The saada paans had no coconut gratings on top and only one clove to pin them up. After adding the drops he had been told to safely dispose of the container. For his services he was given fifty thousand rupees in advance and five lakh were to be given later. He was told not to ask any questions, and there would be no risk to him at all.

The guard did as he was told and after use, he had thrown the container into the deep gutter covered entirely with overgrown grass outside the gate. He'd thought no one would find it. He said that later the police had arrived, found the money in his cupboard and arrested him. He had not left for his village because it would have seemed fishy and he had kept the money in his cupboard since he did not have a bank locker to hide it in.

Dr Dixit, on Ravi's insistence, kept asking whether he had taken Rao's mobile and closed the door from outside, but he kept denying this. His psychoanalysis report also corroborated the polygraph tests. The brain mapping to find out whether he was hiding anything was inconclusive. None of this evidence was, however, permissible in court; but they recorded the whole session and played it back to him afterwards to prove to him that he had confessed his role in the murder.

'Balram Singh, you have revealed the whole truth of your involvement in the case. If you now give us a statement accepting your role in the murder, you will get away with a lighter sentence, otherwise you may have to be in jail for the rest of your life!'

To Ravi and Rahul's delight, the scared guard gave a statement accepting his involvement in the case and assisted the police artist in drawing a portrait of the man who had recruited him, given him the poison container and the advance money.

When he was brought face to face with Rajeev Kabra along with three other men in an identification parade, the guard identified Rajeev Kabra. He also said that if Kabra spoke, he would be 100 per cent sure of his identity. As soon as Rajeev Kabra was made to speak a sentence, the guard quickly said that he was the same man. His rasping voice was unmistakable!

Ravi and Rahul went over the evidence again. The fact that all their doubts were slowly being corroborated motivated them to continue working with vigour.

'Rahul, the case against Rajeev Kabra is getting stronger. We have quite a bit of hard evidence of his role in Rao's murder. But what do we have against Vineet? Since the guard is steadfastly denying any role in taking away and then replacing Rao's mobile, or in locking and then again reopening the door, it has to be Vineet who did this. This had probably been his allotted role.' Rahul nodded.

Ravi said, 'The evidence that we have against Vineet so far is that he was overheard threatening his father once in an argument with him. His driver Ramu had reported this spat between father and son when I had spoken to him and that Vineet was present in the farmhouse when Rao died. His bad relations with his father are widely known. What goes against him further is the fact that he had gone to the farmhouse alone with his father and had the maximum opportunity of murdering him there. But Vineet keeps denying any role in his father's death, and strangely, I have started feeling that he might be telling the truth.'

Rahul grew confused, 'Then chief, who in your opinion was the person involved in meddling with the door and mobile?'

'Maybe it was the caretaker, Rahul. But I feel that the man is innocent. However, law does not work on hunches, so we will have to arrest the caretaker and subject him to the full routine that has been followed with the other three. Arrest him tomorrow Rahul, but I also want you to keep thinking who else could have come to the farmhouse that night.'

'Chief, I'll have to subject my brain to the kind of nocturnal exercises that you subject yours to. Let me try it tonight and see whether the name of the "door and mobile man" can be brought to light!'

Ravi smiled. He was in a good mood ever since the case had been handed back to him.

That night Rahul went to bed with a one-point challenge to his brain—was there someone else present in the farmhouse who could have been involved? His mind repeatedly went over the sequence of events preceding Rao's death. Could it have been one of the farmhands? Unlikely, since they never entered the house. And if they had done so it might have raised suspicion. Were they forgetting some person who was legitimately present there and could have entered and left the house without anyone noticing? His mind was in turmoil all night but towards daybreak it finally dawned on him that there *was* one more person present at the farmhouse that night who had every right to be there! And this person could have easily fabricated an excuse to enter Rao's room. Rahul slept for less than two hours that night but he nevertheless felt euphoric in the morning. Later when he met Ravi at the office he could not stop himself from exclaiming, 'Eureka! I have done it! I've guessed the name of the person who could have been there legitimately.'

Ravi burst out laughing, 'Out with it!'

'Chief, we forgot one man who was also present at the farmhouse that night. The driver who drove the father and son to the farmhouse! I checked with Dilip and he confirmed that it was Rao's driver Ramu!'

'Excellent! How did we miss that? Sometimes we tend to miss the most obvious clue. Send someone and pick up Vineet's driver Nathu first. Let us talk to him before tackling Rao's driver.'

'Yes chief,' replied Rahul excitedly.

~

A scared Nathu was brought to Ravi's office within an hour. Ravi felt it would be easy to get information out of him. Rahul seated him on a chair and told him not to be afraid; they would just ask him a few routine questions. But it was like reassuring a child confronted with a syringe and needle that there would be no pain! The man was sweating so badly that there was danger of his fainting with fear. Ravi thought that due to his background, it was more than likely that he had been interrogated by the police before, and this explained the exaggerated reaction.

Ravi decided to put an end to his suspense, 'We want to question you about someone else, so please relax. Now I will ask you a few things about Ramu, your bade sahib's driver, and you must answer truthfully.' The poor man looked a little relieved but not entirely comfortable.

'Tell us,' Ravi put a hand over his shoulder, 'does Ramu have any bad habits like drinking or gambling?'

'No sir, he is a very religious person and does not indulge in such activities.'

'Do you have any knowledge that he was in need of a large sum of money?'

Nathu hesitated. He was probably contemplating the pros and cons of coming out with the truth. And he was still not certain where all this was leading. He was sure they were out to nail him for some role he had apparently played in the murder, but was not sure what. Ravi was experienced enough to know what was going through the driver's mind.

'If you don't answer quickly, we may have to arrest you. Again let me reassure you that we do not think you are directly involved in the murder we are investigating.'

Nathu now began to speak slowly, his fear not having dissipated fully. He told them that Ramu had recently put in a major sum of his earnings in a money multiplier scheme floated by another driver known to them. After initial returns, this driver had suddenly disappeared, taking away the money of many people like Ramu who had also fallen for the scheme. In fact, Nathu had also wanted to put in money but was always tragically short of it! He said that Ramu was extremely depressed after this and his mind had always been working on how to get his money back, since he wanted to go back to Hyderabad and settle there. After his big sahib's death, he had seemed to become more jittery and restless and had in fact told him only yesterday that he planned to go back to Hyderabad the following week.

Rahul noticed that Ravi was patting his pocket that contained a photo of Gandhiji. That meant he was satisfied.

'Rahul, take Nathu to the waiting room and have someone keep an eye on him. We will let him go once we have tackled Ramu.'

Ravi now rang up Dilip and asked him to come to the police headquarters with Ramu, without alerting him in any way. He gave Dilip an inkling of the driver's involvement in the case. Dilip was there in forty minutes, and just before reaching he called Ravi. Rahul was therefore waiting to escort the driver inside as soon as they reached there.

Ravi decided to go straight for the jugular, 'Be seated Ramu. We had told you that we might seek your cooperation if needed, and we have brought you here for that. I want to ask you a few questions but before that I will tell you what we have found out about you.

'You had put in most of your savings in a money multiplier scheme where you got cheated. You were desperate to get your money back somehow or the other because you wanted to go back to Hyderabad. During this time a man approached you for a small task that was well within your capability and reach. You were probably told not to ask any questions and to just complete the job. For this you were to be paid a large sum of money.' Ravi paused in his narrative, happy to observe the response he was generating in the driver. 'Do you want to tell us about it, or should we arrest you first?'

Ramu remained silent, so Ravi continued, 'Okay . . . you obviously want me to complete the story. Your instructions were to watch out for Vineet. As soon as he left Rao's room, you were to enter on some pretext and take away your boss's mobile, and on the way out you were to bolt his door from outside. Then, exactly six hours later, you had to unbolt the door again and replace the mobile.'

The driver now spoke, 'Sir, you must believe me when I say that I did not know *why* I had to take away sahib's mobile and bolt the door. At least, I did not expect that he would be murdered. I thought that at the most, someone would come and threaten him or talk to him. When I came to know that he died that night, I was very angry with myself.' He paused, before resuming again, 'I was not in the right frame of mind since I had lost a lot of money and could not differentiate between what was right and wrong. I was only thinking about how to get my money back. But if such a godly person has died because of me, please arrest me and give me whatever punishment I deserve.' He then started to weep uncontrollably.

Ravi waited a few minutes and then asked him to give a statement.

'Sir, most of what you have said is correct. I was cheated badly; normally, I am a very God-fearing person who stays away from any kind of wrongdoing. But in the unstable state of mind that I was in, when someone offered to compensate my loss and also give me something extra, greed overtook good sense. I was told that my only job would be to close and then reopen sahib's door at the stated time, and if possible, to remove the mobile and again replace it that night.'

'Okay, so tell us how you did it.'

'I stood outside where I could not be seen, and when I saw chhote sahib leave the room, I waited a few minutes and then gently knocked on bade sahib's door. As there was no response, I walked in. Bade sahib was in the bathroom so I quickly picked up his mobile and put it in my pocket. Then I walked out. I had made up my mind that if anybody saw me, I would tell them that I was waiting to meet bade sahib to ask him what time we would leave in the morning. But no one saw me, so I quietly bolted his door. Then I went back to my small room. I checked the time, it was 9.30 p.m.

'My instructions were to go back exactly six hours later, replace the mobile and unbolt the door. I always keep an alarm clock with me since I have to often wake up at odd hours. I set the alarm for 3 a.m. and slept. When the alarm rang I went to bade sahib's room. I unbolted the door and went in to replace the cellphone that I had carefully wiped to remove my fingerprints and was holding with a kerchief. But as soon as I entered, I got the shock of my life!

'The light was on and bade sahib was on the floor near the bathroom. He looked dead to me. I panicked and rushed out, closing the door after me and leaving it unbolted after throwing the mobile on the bed. I reached my room somehow, sweating profusely and trembling all over. I just hated myself for the fact that I had probably contributed to my master's death. Later in the morning when Dr Reddy declared that the death was natural, I was a little reassured. But the next day I was called to a place far from my master's house, and handed over the money for the part I had played, confirming my suspicion that he had been murdered.'

'Who gave you the money?'

'A man in a driver's uniform who came in a white Honda Accord.'

'Was there anyone else in the car?'

'The driver had stopped the car and walked towards me, but from a distance I could make out that there was a man and a woman inside. However, I could not see them clearly since the windows were tinted.'

'Do you remember the number of the car?'

'Yes, it had a Delhi registration and the number was 10. I remember the number, because I thought the owner must be someone important to own a car with a number like that.'

'How much money did you receive?'

'They gave me the two lakh that I had lost and two lakh more.' Ramu was now trembling.

Ravi continued, 'Would you be able to recognize the person who first spoke to you?'

'He was a tall, fair man wearing dark glasses, and he wore a muffler around his face. Also, his voice was unique. It was a grating voice.'

'Would you be able to recognize the driver and the car?'

'Yes sir, I can never forget them since they killed my sahib and tricked me into helping them!'

'Please sign this statement after adding that you have given it voluntarily and without any pressure from us.'

Ramu signed the statement in broken English.

Ravi then spoke, 'We will have to arrest you and keep you in custody till the charge sheets are filed.'

'That's okay sir. I will do any praaishchit that God wants me to do for my role in my master's death. Going to jail is not enough for me.'

They arrested Ramu and sent him to the lock-up.

Meanwhile, Subba Rao the caretaker had been subjected to a polygraph test, but the man came out clean. They did not have any grounds to retain him in custody, so they let him go.

Later in the day Ravi and Rahul had a chance to meet each other in private. Ravi leaned back on his chair and turned to Rahul, 'People think that investigative work is a glamorous profession but like any other, it is 99 per cent perspiration. Of course, you do need some insight and logic to solve cases, but mostly it is sheer hard work. A successful investigative officer therefore needs all these qualities, but mostly the ability to work long hours and not give up.'

'Chief, you certainly have all the qualities, considering your success rate,' Rahul beamed.

'*Our* success Rahul, not mine alone. Please don't underestimate your contribution. But that's enough of mutual admiration. We need to update the CBI director before we retire for the day. Tomorrow we need to talk to Vineet again and decide whether we can exonerate him completely. That part about the driver being asked to bolt the door proves that they had abandoned the idea of receiving any help from Vineet. Probably he was kept in the dark about the whole conspiracy. Also, we must arrange for an identification parade of the driver with Rajeev Kabra, his driver and the car; and another one with Roop Singh and Vijay Kumar. Come on, let's brief the CBI director. It's time to pay our dues for being granted independence in handling the investigation!'

Seventeen

Ravi and Rahul prepared to meet with the CBI officer, but before they could leave for their appointment an inspector walked in. 'Sir there was a call for you from a private commando. I received the call an hour back.'

He handed a slip of paper to Ravi with a phone number on it. Ravi reprimanded the inspector for not giving him the news immediately, 'You know I do not like delays of any kind!'

He immediately dialled the number. The commando said he had highly sensitive and confidential information that he could give only to him. Ravi told him to come to his office next morning at 9 a.m.

By the time they were through with their meeting with the CBI they were exhausted enough to go home. The next day at nine sharp Kartar Singh, who had been the chief of the commando unit taking care of Gowri Shankar Prasad, the cricket board president, walked in. He was about forty years old, tall, well-built and athletic and had the ease of movement that only people who are very fit have.

As he settled into the chair opposite, Ravi asked him the purpose of his visit.

'Sir, I work for a private security agency. I was the chief of security for Shri Gowri Shankar Prasad when an incident occurred, that may have a bearing on this case. Ten days before the death of Sports Minister S.N. Rao, we followed Prasadji as he drove thirty kilometres on to the Haryana highway. Normally, we are informed about the destination well in advance, but this time we were not told anything. We just had to follow his car blindly which I did not like at all. Exactly thirty kilometres into the highway, Prasadji's car gave the signal to stop. This was highly irregular but I had no option except to comply. Twice before, an attempt on his life had been made by his business rivals, when we were in charge of his security, so I was particularly unhappy about halting on a lonely stretch of the highway.

'Within five minutes a car came near us and stopped. We immediately surrounded it, but Prasadji called me from his mobile, telling me to allow the person to enter his car. I vaguely remembered having seen this person somewhere but could not place him immediately. However, I noted the car number and time and mentally registered his face. The stranger and Prasadji were inside the car for almost half an hour. Even his driver was asked to step out and wait with us. We could not hear what was being said, but the visitor seemed upset. When he finally came out, he looked highly preoccupied, got into his car and drove away. Those thirty minutes were really scary. We were like sitting ducks and anyone could have come and attacked us!'

'Did you discuss this with Gowri Shankar Prasad?'

'Normally, I did not speak to Prasadji but received instructions from his driver, but on that day I felt it was my duty to convey to him the breach in security protocol that had occurred and the risk that was involved. Prasadji just nodded his head and asked us to proceed back to Delhi. I also said that I would have to report the matter to my boss, but he dissuaded me by saying it was a highly sensitive meeting. I reluctantly agreed, but logged in the date and timings in the official log book when we went back. I also wrote down the car number of the visitor. I thought the matter was closed but was taken by surprise when within a few days, I was removed from this highly senior post and appointed at a less important and lower paying one by my boss. I knew who was responsible but could not do anything about it.'

'Have you found out the identity of the person who met Mr Prasad that day? It is crucial and will help us understand why this happened with you.'

The tall, well-built guard shifted a little in his seat, 'I was coming to that sir. When the news of S.N. Rao's death broke, followed by the arrest of his own son on suspicion of murder, I immediately recognized Vineet as the person who had met Prasadji on the highway that day, and thought that the incident may have some significance. I have been debating in my mind since then about what action to take. And then I came to know that you were in charge of the case. For the past two days I have been trying to call you and finally yesterday I got through to your inspector.'

There he goes! thought Rahul as Ravi patted his shirt pocket. The chief is happy! Rahul himself could hardly suppress his excitement. They were actually getting evidence that the board president could also be involved. Things were really heating up!

Ravi said, 'What you've told us is extremely significant and I want to congratulate and thank you for doing your duty.'

'Sir, I want to remind you that I had logged in the car number and the time of the meeting in the official logbook. The entry should be there unless it has been deleted.'

Ravi called his inspector and asked him to go to the office of the commando unit. He said he should ask for the logbook relating to the date and time of the meeting and bring it to him. If anyone objected, he should call him and he would talk to the person. He then handed the inspector an authority letter with his seal and sent him on his way.

He now turned to Kartar Singh, 'Thank you again for doing your duty and helping us in our investigation.'

Kartar Singh saluted and departed, his anger at having been demoted for doing his duty, slightly assuaged.

'There you have it Rahul, evidence of Vineet's and, more importantly, a *probability* of Gowri Shankar Prasad's involvement. This is really big! The board president himself may be heading the whole conspiracy! Kartar Singh has really provided us with a lucky break. Let us get official confirmation from the logbook and then confront Vineet. We were going to totally exonerate him, and now this evidence emerges. And as for Prasad, we will have to speak to Rajeev Kabra again and get him to implicate the board president as well as Hansraj Verma.'

Rahul said, 'Chief, the first little trail we found ourselves on when we went to the farmhouse, bifurcated into many divergent ones; but I feel they are all now re-converging towards the lane that will now take us to a target we never dreamt of—Gowri Shankar Prasad!'

'That was well put Rahul. We do have the first bit of direct evidence that Gowri Shankar Prasad is also involved. Hopefully, when we confront Vineet tomorrow or Rajeev Kabra later, we will get something more.'

Within an hour, the inspector returned with photocopies from the official logbook, pertaining to the meeting on the highway, from the commando office.

'Rahul, get me an intelligence update on Gowri Shankar Prasad. We need to read up on him.'

A little later, Rahul came back with a thick file. They learnt that the president, Gowri Shankar Prasad was an ambitious man. Although he had grown up in a village, he had done everything to find his way out.

He got into every kind of business that could earn him money. Money by itself had not attracted him, but it was a conduit to power and therefore, indispensable. He had married well too and rapidly risen to become one of the most powerful and rich people in the Indian industry. Of course, all obstacles in his path to progress were cleared by the two politicians in his family, his brother and his father-in-law. They learnt that he had first formed a support base for himself in his home state of Haryana and then become the head of the state cricket board. Then when he was eligible to stand for elections to the central board, he had canvassed amongst the members of the existing board and offered them huge incentives to get himself elected. Later, when elections were held for the post of board president, the mandate was clear. He was elected unopposed.

'Prasad has three daughters, who are all married now. Two of them are doctors, staying abroad and one is living with him. His brother, Raj Shankar Prasad is at present the leader of a major opposition party.'

Ravi spoke up, 'What an amazing personality, Rahul, you have to admire him for his meteoric rise. Ironically, I am not going to enjoy bringing him down if he is really involved in the murders.'

Next day, Ravi and Rahul went to question Vineet again. Warned by Ravi's reputation Vineet had his lawyer by his side. Ravi began by telling him what they had found out. 'We have come to know that you had a secret meeting with Gowri Shankar Prasad on the highway that has been officially recorded. This is your last chance to tell us the truth.'

Vineet had a whispered consultation with his lawyer who nodded, apparently giving him the go ahead to speak the truth.

Vineet began, 'I was approached by Rajeev Kabra about ten days before my father died, saying that Gowri Shankar Prasad would like to meet me. He said there was a way of resolving the differences between my father and me and also clearing off all my debts. He even hinted at the possibility of my being offered membership of the cricket board. I was excited and decided to meet Mr Prasad as per their plan.

'When I entered his car, he beat about the bush for some time, trying to gauge how bad the relations between my father and me were. Then he told me that my dad was proving a hindrance to their plans by his moralistic attitude and would I join them in trying to remove him. If I helped them, they would get me into the board in my father's place and also clear off my debts. I promise you that when he said "remove" I thought it was only from the board and had not the remotest inkling that he meant taking my father's life.'

'What happened next?'

'Mr Prasad then started speaking ill of my father. I know I have behaved badly with my dad in the past, but when anyone else speaks ill of him, I do not like it. However, being the weak person that I am, I kept quiet. But then he said, "I think you have understood what I am hinting at and will play a role in it." I was getting uneasy and confused, and blurted out that I needed time to ponder over what he had said.

'His next words were, "If you decide not to come all out in our support, consider this meeting never happened, but if you do decide to help, we are here to take care of your future."

'I just got out of the car and walked out. Later I thought hard about the meeting and decided that Mr Prasad was a very dangerous man and it was best that I kept away from him.

'Therefore, when I received SMSes from Rajeev Kabra, I gave non-committal responses and tried to forget about the whole episode.

'Then I went to the farmhouse with my father where he tried to counsel me regarding my addictions. I had become very adept at handling situations like this. I promised that I would cooperate with him in every way but had no real intention of doing so. I haven't been a good son to him, but you must believe me when I say that I had absolutely no role in his death, and do not know how it happened. I would have treated him better had I known what was going to happen to him. When I was arrested, I felt I deserved it in some way although I had nothing to do with it.'

'I hope you are telling the truth, and if we are able to verify that you are, we will ensure that you are released soon.'

After Vineet was taken away again, Ravi turned to Rahul, 'Gowri Shankar Prasad has been very clever. He did not speak anything directly to Vineet but let him read between the lines. And when he felt that he would probably not cooperate, he got Rajeev Kabra to rope in Rao's driver Ramu and the security guard Balram Singh into the conspiracy. Each probably did not know that the other was also involved. They had done their homework well, perhaps through Ace Detective Agency again. They knew that both these guys needed money and would prove easy bait. And by hiring them, they were able to bypass Vineet completely. Also, the board president has kept himself in the background and we may not have found out anything about his role in Rao's murder, if it had not been for Kartar Singh.'

'Chief, should we inform the CBI about this development?' Rahul asked.

'No Rahul, let us wait till we have enough evidence to nail him before talking to them.'

But before they could proceed further, a second death occurred at Yashodhan. This death would provide the missing evidence, to link Rajeev Kabra to Sunanda's murder.

~

Neela had decided to quit her job and stay at home so that she could take care of Shweta, but she remained under tremendous stress because of her sister's antagonistic attitude towards her, and could not sleep at night. Sanjay had to start giving her sedatives. This helped her to sleep soundly, but she would wake up only around 7 a.m., whereas her normal waking time was five. They had managed to get another nurse who Shweta tolerated better than she did her sister but she came only in the daytime.

On 9 October, Neela woke up early at three in the morning as she had forgotten to take her sedative. Some noise had woken her up. She went to the bathroom where there was a strong smell of vomit. Maybe Sanjay had thrown up at night she thought. However, he seemed to be sleeping peacefully so he was probably all right. Neela again went back to sleep although it was fitful and got up once more at five. She now decided to go up and check on Shweta.

When she opened her sister's room, she pulled back in consternation! Shweta was lying on the floor. She was clutching her precious banyan bonsai that had been broken, and there was a smell of vomit in the room. Neela immediately knew Shweta was dead, and felt numb with shock for a minute, but she knew she must fetch Sanjay to take a look at her. If there was even a remote possibility that Shweta could be revived, it had to be tried! With great difficulty she managed to pull herself together and ran down to call Sanjay.

'Sanjay, get up, something bad has happened to Shweta!' she said, shaking him vigorously.

Sanjay jumped up, and ran up with Neela. While Sanjay was examining Shweta, Neela also rang up Ravi and told him about the death of her sister. She did not know why she was calling him but felt she had to. Sanjay declared that Shweta had died several hours earlier. He pulled Neela away from the room, took her downstairs and gave her some water, and tried to comfort her.

'Neela, Shweta is no more. She seems to have taken an overdose of her anti-psychotic medicines. I don't know if it was a good idea calling the police, we could have quietly cremated her.'

'Sanjay,' Neela replied, 'since Sunanda's death, I really don't want to take any kind of chance. Let the police decide what's to be done.'

'As you wish, the decision is yours,' Sanjay replied with a sigh.

~

Ravi rushed to Yashodhan with an ambulance, and removed the body for post-mortem. Poor Shweta, he thought, she looks beautiful even in death. Meanwhile, Rahul also arrived and took the statements of Neela and Sanjay and left. But before leaving, he made a note of the freshly washed pyjama suit still dripping, and hung out on the shower curtain rod in the master bathroom.

During the post-mortem Shweta's stomach contents and blood samples were preserved and sent for forensic examination. The same question remained: murder or suicide?

Ravi realized that it was time to act fast. A week after Shweta's death he decided to talk to Neela in private without Sanjay being present. He knew Neela was in shock and he might not be able to elicit much from her, but he had to give it a try. When he met her, he saw that she seemed to have lost weight and was not her usual self.

Why was she so nervous and edgy? What was she hiding? To put her at ease, Ravi told her that he would do the talking and she only had to listen. In the end he might put a few questions to her.

He narrated the sequence of events as he knew them till date, and slowly Neela's eyes turned to him. 'I am going to now reveal something that might hurt you—Sanjay and Sunanda were in a relationship before he got married to you. Unfortunately, this continued even after the marriage.'

Neela did not look shocked at all. *So the liftman in Sanjay's building had been right!* Neela clearly had an inkling of it.

He continued, 'Sanjay was probably helping Sunanda financially, we've found out that he was depositing big amounts into the joint account that he held with her.'

Neela still kept silent and did not respond so Ravi went on with his revelations, 'Sunanda was also seeing another person. You might have heard of him—Rajeev Kabra, who is a member of the cricket board. She knew him since the days she was taking care of his mother who was a patient of Alzheimer's disease. After she passed away, Sunanda had come to your house to take care of Shweta. In fact, your sister has also met him a few times along with Sunanda.' Neela just nodded and continued to remain silent.

'Now, this part of my revelation might affect you deeply, but I have to say it. Sanjay's charm had worked its magic on Shweta too who had also fallen for him.'

This time Neela was surprised. 'How did you discover this?' she asked. He told Neela about the banyan bonsai root message Rahul had accidentally come across in Shweta's room, and their interpretation of it. He drew it for her—

S♡S

'This probably meant—"Shweta loves Sanjay".'

Suddenly, Neela started crying quietly and the tears flowed unchecked down her face. All her vaunted poise had left her. The bottled up emotions kept flowing for a full ten minutes, before the tide ebbed.

Finally she spoke, 'I am sorry for breaking down like this, but I couldn't help it. I have forced myself to remain strong and under control, but too many things have happened in too short a time. I knew about the affair that Sanjay was having with Sunanda, since I had seen them once in a compromising position. But I did not want to jeopardize our marriage. Regarding Shweta's love for Sanjay, I had an inkling of that too, but did not believe it was anything serious.'

Ravi looked straight into her eyes and asked, 'Did you murder Sunanda or Shweta?'

'I did not murder Sunanda, and could never ever murder Shweta since I loved her very much and considered myself her protector.' Her eyes were steady as she looked straight at him and he felt she was telling the truth.

'You want to tell me anything else?' Ravi asked cautiously.

Neela continued sitting, looking down at the ground as if wanting to speak more, but instead of saying anything, she just sighed.

Ravi felt that she wanted to reveal something important but did not push her. In the evening he called Rahul and updated him on his meeting with Neela.

'I want to speak to Sanjay again, let's catch up with him tomorrow at nine, before he leaves for his consultation.'

~

Both reached Yashodhan early morning the next day. They were in civilian clothes and had come in Ravi's car. Sanjay was having breakfast while Neela was trying to read the papers. When the two police officers entered, both seemed startled. Neela, however, quickly recovered and requested them to be seated.

Ravi began, 'I want to update both of you on what we know so far. You, Dr Nanda, started your practice at Karol Bagh after your MD. Soon after that, Sunanda came into your life as a young receptionist and nurse. She was the only person whom you truly loved before and even after your marriage to Neela, which was one of convenience.'

Sanjay's eyes were angry and his forehead furrowed, but he did not speak. Neela's eyes, however, dropped and she looked down.

Ravi felt bad for her but continued, 'You got Sunanda into the house to take care of Shweta, so that you could meet her whenever you wanted.' Sanjay quickly looked at Neela, but she was still gazing at the ground and did not react.

The story went on: 'Since you were married to Neela, you had to naturally spend a lot of time with her and that made Sunanda jealous. The plan had been to get as much money out of Neela as possible, divorce her and then marry Sunanda. You, therefore, asked Neela to act as guarantor for the 1.3 crore loan you needed to buy the South Delhi clinic and procured it from the bank with her help. You also had a joint account with Sunanda in the bank into which you were depositing big amounts every month.'

Sanjay's eyebrows went up but he continued to keep his mouth shut.

'Things seemed to continue smoothly for a year, before Sunanda started pressurizing you to divorce Neela quickly and marry her since her parents wanted her to settle down soon. You, on the other hand, were finding it difficult to pay the heavy monthly instalments for your clinic, and you decided that remaining married to Neela was a more lucrative option. So you planned and carried out Sunanda's death as an "accident".'

Sanjay stood up, unable to control himself any further, 'Neela, this police officer is talking total rubbish! Please don't believe a word of what he has said. He is somehow trying to extract a confession out of one of us and we should not fall into his trap.'

Before he could continue, Ravi loudly and very firmly asked him to sit down and let him complete his narrative, 'I will give you an opportunity to speak later.' Sanjay looked extremely angry but sat down sullenly.

Ravi now described in detail Shweta's occupation with the bonsais, and Rahul's meeting with her that had revealed that she too was in love with Sanjay. Sanjay's brows knit up and he closed his eyes before opening them again. Even a trained psychiatrist like him could not hide his emotions.

Ravi kept up the relentless pressure, 'Shweta had become desperate for your attention and probably revealed innocently that she knew you had murdered Sunanda. This made you decide to do away with her too.' Sanjay clenched his fists again tightly in an attempt to hold on to his emotions.

Giving him no respite, Ravi continued, 'You had gone to meet Shweta at night, and probably given her a glass of milk with enough medication to prove lethal. Shweta had vomited all over the room but enough of the drugs had been absorbed into her bloodstream to kill her. Or had you also given her an injection? The post-mortem report has revealed lethal doses of anti-psychotic medication in her blood.'

Sanjay suddenly laughed, 'Theories, all theories, totally untrue and they'll get you nowhere!'

Ravi looked Sanjay directly in his eyes, 'I have enough evidence to arrest you and if you do not cooperate, I will have to do so.'

'DCP Sharma, you cannot browbeat me into confessing to crimes I did not commit. I know my rights and will call my lawyer now.'

'Please go ahead. But ask him to come to the police station where we are going to escort you!' Ravi shot back.

Sanjay gave a call to Anand Bhatia, his lawyer, and explained the situation briefly, requesting him to come to the police station immediately. Though Bhatia was in a hearing, he handed over the case to his junior and rushed there, a little after the police officers reached. Meanwhile, the media had got a whiff and started gathering outside, expecting some kind of breakthrough. The word must have somehow got around that Dr Sanjay Nanda had been arrested. The lawyer had to fight his way through them, helped by Rahul who rushed out when he heard the commotion. Once inside, Bhatia shook hands with Ravi who he knew and respected. 'DCP Sharma, give me ten minutes in private with my client and then he will give a statement.'

'Please go ahead. You can use the neighbouring room.'

The lawyer escorted his client to the next room and closed the door. They returned in half an hour to the room where Ravi and Rahul were waiting for them. Sanjay now began talking and Rahul recorded his statement, 'Sunanda was just a friend and an employee. It is not true that we were having an affair. I love my wife and that is why I married her.'

Ravi did not respond, although he did not miss the fact that his lawyer's eyebrows had shot up. Sanjay studiously ignored his lawyer and continued, 'As far as Shweta was concerned, she had been infatuated with me and whenever I visited her she would try to get close.'

Sanjay's speech was measured as if he was thinking before speaking each word. He now paused and Ravi had to force him to continue.

'I need time to collect my thoughts.'

'Okay, we are prepared to wait.'

Ravi did not want to force anything out of Sanjay, so he chose to be patient. But after some time he again prodded Sanjay to speak.

'I . . . I . . .' Sanjay continued to stutter.

Ravi now decided to ask direct questions, 'What do you remember of the happenings on 30 August, the day Sunanda died?'

The pain resurfaced in Sanjay's eyes when he heard Sunanda's name.

'That morning had been a routine one. In the afternoon around 1 p.m. I came home, had a quick lunch and left.'

'Was this usual?'

'No,' said Sanjay. 'This was not usual but I had to collect some important papers so I combined that with lunch.'

'Did you meet Sunanda?'

'Yes, I saw her briefly since she came down to serve me lunch.'

'Is it not true that you often came home to be with Sunanda?'

'No, that is an absolute untruth!'

'Did you go back to the house again after about two hours on that day?'

'No,' Sanjay said firmly. 'I went home only when Neela called me with the news of Sunanda's death.' Suddenly Sanjay's shoulders started shaking. He covered his face for some time. The three men waited patiently for him to regain control. After some time he pulled himself together and said, 'Sorry gentlemen, Sunanda was a good friend and employee and I am yet to get over her loss.' He sighed again and became quiet.

Ravi allowed him a few minutes of respite and then began again, 'Now, coming to the night of 9 October when Shweta died. What do you recollect?'

Sanjay was meant to confess but developed cold feet, 'I came to know of Shweta's death only when Neela woke me up after discovering her body.'

Bhatia had an openly disapproving look on his face, but kept quiet.

Ravi noted this but did not react. He quietly concluded the proceedings by saying, 'Then it's okay. You say you were not involved in either of the deaths. Hereon it is for us to find out the truth. Please sign the statement you have just made.'

Ravi and Rahul decided to talk to Neela who had accompanied her husband to the police station and was waiting in an adjoining room. On seeing her, Ravi again had the feeling that she was innocent. He told her that they had just spoken to Sanjay and he said he had not committed any murder and now they wanted to speak to her.

'Did you know that the relationship between Sanjay and Sunanda went beyond that of an employer and employee?'

Tears welled up in Neela's eyes as she said in a broken voice, 'They were deeply in love with each other, and I found that out on discovering them in a compromising position as I had told you earlier. Sanjay did not know I had seen them.'

Ravi nodded and then asked, 'Who killed Sunanda? Or was it an accident?'

Neela opened her purse and quietly handed over a letter. 'I think it's high time I gave you this.' It was written in a neat, small and even handwriting. 'Shweta's,' said Neela.

Dear Neela, you were always the lucky one. You got Sanjay, whom I love too. I'm very jealous and almost hate you. But recently I discovered that Sunanda too loves Sanjay and I could not bear that. I saw them twice in each other's arms and had been mad at her since then.

On 27 August, Sunanda and I went to the park, where her friend Mr Kabra also came. When Sunanda went to get me an ice-cream, he told me that she had changed totally and wasn't his friend any more. He said she seemed to care more for Sanjay than for him, in spite of all the financial help he had given her. I told him that I also did not like her any more as I had seen her many times with Sanjay. He smiled and said we both were friends and told me what I should do.

A few days earlier, Sunanda had examined my banyan bonsai and probably discovered my love for Sanjay. Since she knew my secret I started hating her even more. On the 30th when she again went near the banyan, I was furious. I remembered the advice Mr Kabra had given me. I asked her for some milk and when she was going downstairs to get it, I followed her and pushed her very hard with the extra curtain rod in my room. She fell down the stairs and her neck twisted to one side. I went down to see her, but I think she died immediately, because she did not move at all! Now she can never get Sanjay. I'm telling you this because although I do not like you very much, you are still my sister—Shweta.

Neela explained, 'I have been carrying this letter in my purse with a lot of guilt since Sunanda's death. My poor, confused and sick Shweta, she never knew what she was doing. Maybe I should have shown this to you earlier.'

Ravi looked at her contemplatively and said, 'What about Shweta's death? Who killed her? It could only be you or Sanjay.'

'I think Shweta's death was a suicide. There were many thoughts raging in her mind—joy, love, remorse, hatred, and she was slowly moving towards a severe relapse in her condition. She was not conscious of what she was doing and in a fit of depression, probably consumed about twenty-thirty tablets of her anti-psychotic medication. She then broke her banyan bonsai and as the effect of the medication took place, vomited and collapsed before help could reach her. My poor Shweta! Maybe it was good she died before she deteriorated further. I always want to remember her as she was when our parents were alive—so pretty and innocent.' Neela's voice was now almost a whisper. Tears welled up again in her eyes as she could not control herself.

'Well,' said Ravi, 'that lets Sanjay off. So he was speaking the truth. Madam, come to my office, and let's conclude the proceedings. But before that please sign this statement.'

They went back to the office where Sanjay and his lawyer were waiting. Ravi turned to the lawyer, 'Your client seems to be innocent, Mr Bhatia. We have no case against him. Good day!'

Both Bhatia and Sanjay looked surprised but relieved. The waiting media surrounded them, but they got away saying he was innocent.

Rahul looked shocked. 'Chief,' he said, 'there's something wrong somewhere. I think a lot of lies are being told and if I could spot it, I'm sure you definitely did too.'

Ravi gave an amused smile and patted Rahul on the back, 'Trust me. Sometimes you have to play games. You give people a lot of rope and wait till they entangle themselves. Just be patient. You'll know the truth!'

Eighteen

Two days later, Ravi called Neela and told her he wanted to see her alone.

Neela answered, 'Mr Sharma, please come at eleven, my husband would have left by then.'

When Ravi saw Neela the next day, she was looking outwardly serene but could barely hide her tension. The two deaths followed by all the media attention she was getting was pulling her down. Ravi knew his plan was working.

He casually asked, 'Everything okay between Sanjay and you?'

Neela toyed with her wrist watch but said nothing.

'Ready to talk or you want me to do so?' Ravi asked again.

Neela gave a strained smile and began to speak, 'I wanted to save him thinking there was no point in wasting his life in jail. He had suffered enough since he loved Sunanda and had lost her. I thought we could pick up the bits and pieces of our lives and continue from here. But he has changed totally and the mask is off. He wants only my money and now that he thinks the case against him is closed, he has become openly rude. He wants me to clear off the loan he has taken from the bank since according to him he is finding it difficult to pay the instalments. I have told him that I'll review the balance in my accounts and see what can be done, but I don't like it. And . . .' she paused.

'Go ahead, unburden yourself. Tell me everything and then if you feel like it, give an official statement. I'll then tackle Sanjay. Start from the beginning and tell the whole truth this time,' Ravi instructed.

'You know most of it. After our parents' death, I felt completely responsible towards Shweta although she was elder to me, and when she started behaving strangely, one of my colleagues at office recommended Sanjay. She said her mother had taken his treatment and was to a large extent stable now. Sanjay agreed to a home visit and his treatment helped Shweta a lot. Within a week she was better. But since we could afford it, Sanjay suggested I get a full-time caretaker and sent Sunanda to us.

'After this we saw each other frequently and he is so handsome and competent that when he proposed marriage, I felt flattered and immediately agreed. Things seemed very normal for a few months so when he requested that I give my name as a guarantor for the loan he needed to move into a new office, I agreed. Once or twice I caught him with Sunanda and the relationship seemed more than that of an employer and employee. But I thought he was just flirting. I am a person who loves peace at any cost, and I thought confronting him would only spoil things.

'Then Sunanda died. I discovered the body. The next day Shweta gave me the letter that I showed you and I got all mixed up. I just could not bring myself to reveal that my sister had killed Sunanda. I did not know what to do. I left my job and decided to be available for Shweta twenty-four hours. But she was antagonistic towards me. Increasingly, it was only Sanjay whom she listened to and obeyed.

'Then on the night of 9 October, Shweta died too. Recently, I had started taking sedatives to get sleep, but forgot my dose on that particular day. Two things happened that night: around 3 a.m., I got up as some noise had disturbed me. Sanjay seemed to be sleeping soundly, but the bathroom light was on, so I went to switch it off. There I got a distinct smell of vomit and I thought Sanjay had thrown up at night. I also saw a rolled up towel and a set of his nightclothes. I went off to sleep again although it was fitful.

'I got up at 5 a.m. once more and decided to check whether Shweta was okay and discovered her body. Seeing that Shweta had vomited all over the room, and having discovered his clothes in the bathroom that smelt of vomit, I could guess that Sanjay had a hand in Shweta's death. Later, I casually asked him if he had woken up early in the morning because he was unwell, but he firmly denied it. He also quickly washed his towel and pyjama set when he knew the police was on its way.' She looked at Ravi.

Ravi spoke, 'I have enough evidence to arrest him and will do so. Neela, do you have any evidence to prove that he asked you to pay off the clinic loan?'

'Yes, I went to our main bank at Greater Kailash and also had a meeting with Mr Mehra along with Sanjay. To both, we explained the situation, and they said they would see what could be done. Mr Mehra's advice was to give him at least three months so that he could liquidate only those stocks that would fetch us a profit. So both Mr Mehra and Mr Ganesan, the manager of the bank, are aware of the facts.'

'Excellent!' said Ravi. 'I'm going to do it properly this time. Rahul and I will work overtime today to prepare the case and charge sheet. Tomorrow we will arrest him. You don't worry about anything and don't hesitate to call me at any hour. And also, keep your cellphone close to you always.'

Neela thanked Ravi. She felt a load off her mind after telling him the truth, and was content to leave things in his capable hands.

Next day at 9 a.m. sharp, Ravi and Rahul arrested Sanjay. They denied his request that he be allowed to meet Neela.

Because of the media interest it generated, the news was out on all the channels within the hour. Sanjay kept denying all charges to the media and said they would have to release him soon. Ravi did not talk much and Rahul would not open his mouth until his boss told him to do so. At Ravi's request, Neela also refused all interviews.

They now had evidence that it was Rajeev Kabra who had instigated Shweta to murder Sunanda. But Ravi continued to be unhappy at not being able to get enough direct evidence to nail their biggest target, Gowri Shankar Prasad.

He decided to persuade Rajeev Kabra to come clean on Prasad and Hansraj Verma, and found him in a mellower mood than before when he went to tackle him.

'I have come to tell you about the progress we've made in your case and also the proof we have collected in some other cases in which you are involved. Let me start from the beginning and tell you the whole story:

'Your first victim was Mane. By yours I mean to include other members of the board too. So far we have ample proof against you and some against Hansraj Verma and Gowri Shankar Prasad. You knew that he was trying to stage a comeback. There was too much money at stake to risk a battle, with even the remotest possibility of his managing to oust you guys and becoming the treasurer, or even the president, or to ride piggyback on someone else to control the board by proxy. Then you hired Ace Detective Agency to find out about his itinerary, and when you came to know about his proposed stay at his Delhi home, your plan was ready.

'You obtained aconite tincture, a common cattle poison, from your village, inducted Mane's servant Vijay Kumar as your accomplice, and had him administer the poison to your victim in a glass of Bloody Mary. The servant also managed to take away his mobile and locked the door from outside, so Mane could not seek help. You knew there was no landline in the house.'

Rajeev Kabra was listening with a totally expressionless face. Ravi had paused but continued again, 'Everything went smoothly. Dr Sobti certified that the death was due to a heart attack and Vijay Kumar left for his hometown Lucknow after collecting his "fees".

'But one inadvertent mistake was made. You sent a congratulatory mail to S.N. Rao instead of one of your co-conspirators. You were unlucky that we found that mail.

'Rao was already giving you guys a hard time with his moralistic attitude, and you felt that if he found out about your role in Mane's "operation", he would be unstoppable. Strangely, he kept quiet about the mail, but you people probably felt that Rao was trying to come to a decision as to what action to take. So it was too much of a risk to let him live.

'It was back to Ace Detective Agency, this time to find out Rao's itinerary for the next month. You found out about his souring relations with his elder son Vineet and tried to induct the latter into the plan to eliminate him. When Vineet did not appear to understand what Gowri Shankar Prasad was getting at, you hired two low-level employees of Rao who were in need of quick money—one to add the poison aconite again? Tested and tried! And the other to lock the door and take away the mobile. Same plan but different victim and different venue. Again the plan succeeded.

'But before this, Rupali a lecturer giving tuitions to your daughter overheard your plans for eliminating the sports minister. She told her sister about this incident and what she had heard. She also said that the next day she was asked to give up her tuition assignment. You people did not know how much she had heard, but you could not take a chance. You found out that her relations with her husband were bad, and in all probability he would be blamed for her death. This time you used a person who you thought no one would suspect—the milkman! He had a legitimate reason to be there early in the morning. This murder was also well-planned and went off well.

'But now a new complication, your girlfriend Sunanda had found out too much. She had started putting two and two together, and was asking too many inconvenient questions. Your answer to this problem: use Shweta to get rid of her. You had to just put the idea into her head and if it failed, you could try something else.

'Now you must be wondering how we found out all this. Well, some of it was due to luck and some due to sheer hard work. But you can see that we know almost everything. Someday I'll tell you the whole story. I am going to leave you now to think over what I have told you, and decide what you want to do. You can contact me whenever you decide your future course of action.'

After the meeting with Kabra, Ravi and Rahul held a review session.

'Rahul, what do you think, will he crack?'

'Chief, he's a tough person, and there's a 50-50 chance that he will weather it out. I wish we had *some* bit of evidence that could shock him out of his silence and make him come clean!'

'I've been thinking along the same lines Rahul, but I've been wracking my brains and not been ... wait a minute, we may still find what we want!'

'How and where chief?'

'We examine his e-mails! But before that, Rahul, call up "Snoopy" from intelligence,' Ravi said urgently.

A smile spread across Rahul's face. Inspector Awasthi was nicknamed Snoopy because he could snoop out any information they wanted and faster than Arora of Ace Detective Agency!

Ravi continued, 'Ask him to immediately to go to the board office and find out Rajeev Kabra's email IDs, birth and marriage anniversary dates and call either of us on our cellphones as fast as possible.'

'Chief, I don't understand what you are getting at.'

'Rahul, I was reading somewhere that most people still use commonly remembered numbers as passwords. All we have to do is get Rajeev Kabra's email IDs, and once we get those, we should be able to open up his mails or get the official hacker to help us do so. If we have all the likely passwords he can use, which will probably be one of the numbers we are seeking, I am hopeful we will be able to open Kabra's mails and get something incriminating there.'

'Good thinking chief!'

The two police officers thought they would have to wait at least an hour but Awasthi walked in fifteen minutes later and casually handed over a piece of paper with not only the information they had asked for, but also Rajeev Kabra's mobile numbers, phone numbers, the numbers of his cars and also his house number!

Ravi smiled at him, 'That was quick and thanks for the rest of the numbers. How did you do it so fast?'

'I don't need to move out of my chair to get information,' replied Snoopy cheekily. 'I let my fingers do all the travelling.'

'Thanks, maybe next time before I go running all over the place gathering evidence and information, I'll come to you first,' Ravi replied, pleased.

'Any time sir!' said Inspector Awasthi before saluting and departing.

'He just called up some contacts he has in the cricket board on the phone and got the information,' said Rahul, laughing.

Ravi now booted his PC and they accessed Kabra's mails, all of which luckily had the same password—his marriage anniversary date! So they didn't need the police hacker after all.

Soon what they saw in the emails gave them a hint as to who the intended recipient of the mail sent by Kabra had been, which had mistakenly landed up in S.N. Rao's mailbox with such disastrous consequences.

'Chief, we've probably been going after the wrong targets entirely!'

'Rahul, let's meet Kabra again, this time handling him is going to be easier.'

~

After Ravi had left him, Rajeev Kabra had plenty of time for introspection. Kabra was in a quandary. DCP Ravi had a formidable reputation that could not be wished away. It had come as a surprise to him as to how quickly and efficiently he had almost solved all the cases. It was only a matter of time before he would get to the whole truth. His mentor had been sending feelers that the evidence of his involvement was very strong in all the cases, and he could not escape, so why not play ball and not implicate him? Then, when things cooled down, he would arrange to bring Kabra out of prison and ensure that his name and reputation were restored.

If Kabra kept quiet, he would have to take the major blame that could even lead to a life sentence or worse. On the other hand, if he told the whole truth his mentor would be implicated. And Kabra had been promised rich financial dividends if he kept his mouth shut; he stood to lose all that money if he opened up. And maybe his mentor *would* be able to get him out in a couple of years. He spent the next few hours debating in his mind what action to take. But the decision was taken out of his hands when Ravi and Rahul walked in. *Why were they coming back? It could only mean they had found out something more!*

'Good afternoon Mr Kabra!' said Ravi, and the hearty greeting deepened Kabra's fears.

'I have come back to complete the story. Now you have two options—either you can listen or complete it for me, which do you prefer?'

Rajeev Kabra just kept silent.

'Okay, since you still prefer silence, let me continue to speak. Rahul and I have been very busy since we left you in the morning. We've been doing some clerical work for you. You haven't been able to check your mails, so we did that for you and they have revealed quite a story.'

Suddenly Ravi turned grim and his voice was steely, 'You and your mentor have been playing lot of games with the police. The whole conspiracy was hatched between the two of you. And he continued to play games even after your arrest. He used Ajay Shukla very cleverly to throw a lot of red herrings in our path, and we were led astray for a while. I think you know who I am talking about—Ramesh Patel!

'We found quite a few exchanges between you and Patel in your mailbox. You had probably deleted most of the interesting ones, but one significant mail still remained—"money deposited in bank". To my mind, people like Ramesh Patel "deposit" money for others in only one kind of bank, the Swiss bank. And can you explain your interaction with the man who is supposedly your worst enemy?'

Rajeev Kabra continued to maintain silence.

'Look, I can find out everything without your help, you know that by now, but we will save some time if you tell me the whole story. Also, we may be able to nip in the bud any further mischief Patel is planning. And by helping the police, the court may view your role in the entire conspiracy with a more lenient eye. So, do you want to confess?'

'Yes,' said Rajeev Kabra, and finally began to speak. 'I came in contact with Hansraj Verma and Gowri Shankar Prasad as the head of my state board. From the very beginning they took a liking to me. Slowly our relationship grew and they promised to get me inducted into the national board as a member. They lived up to their promise and when a vacancy had been created by them, they got me voted in. But I could sense that S.N. Rao was not very happy with me.

'Then Surya had the idea of starting a Twenty20 league and they launched it with much fanfare. Prasad and Verma felt that Surya's league had to be destroyed from purely a business point of view, and we went about doing so. But Rao did not like what was happening and voiced his displeasure. For some reason he disliked me and made it obvious every time we met.' He sighed and stopped for a moment.

'Later in June, we felt the official board should also come out with its own league. Surya had given us the blueprint when he had organized TLI; we only had to elaborate on it. The rest of the board members were also for it. So we went full-tilt and launched our league which proved a huge success.

'But I had to work very hard in organizing it and was upset when the chairmanship of ITL that I thought should have rightfully belonged to me, was handed on a plate to Manik Jindal.'

He paused again and then continued, 'I was extremely disappointed when I was not made the chairman. I was the one who had to do all the hard work, but Manik Jindal was made to head it. Outwardly I pretended to be happy, but from inside I was fuming. I was also unhappy that the major amount of unaccounted money received as kickbacks during ITL was being shared by the two kingpins, and only a little bit here and there was thrown at the rest of us.

'It was when I was in this state of mind that I was approached by Mr Ramesh Patel. He said he was out to avenge the financial and emotional drubbing he had received at the hands of the board and he was prepared to go to any length to achieve his ends. He said he had come to know that I was also upset at the treatment being meted out to me and asked me if I would join him. He said I could continue to be a board member and get paid for any "assistance" I rendered. I agreed to Patel's proposal. He gave me an "advance" of 2.5 crore rupees which he arranged to deposit in my Swiss account.

'But his target was strangely Sunil Mane, supposedly a friend of his. He told me Mane had borrowed a large sum of money from him after his ouster from the board. He was not able or unwilling to pay this back in spite of repeated requests from Patel, but had pledged a huge property in Mumbai to him in lieu of the money he owed. Mane had thought TLI would be a big success and he could pay back his loan, but the board sabotaged it. After the TLI fiasco, Mane flatly refused to return any money.

'Patel roped me in to get rid of Mane. I do not know whether the Mumbai property was an incentive or there was some other reason. I knew this detective called Arora whom I had used many times in the past. I therefore approached him secretly to prepare a dossier on Mane, including his travel plans for the next month. We came to know that he would be staying at his Delhi home on 9 and 10 August.

Coming from a village background I know a little about cattle poisons. There is a good man in my village who sells stuff like this, how you ever found out about him, I do not know! From him I easily procured the poison and learnt how to use it.

'Ramesh Patel met Mane on 10 August, along with Surya Seth, on the pretext of planning their revenge against the board. But the plan to murder Mane instead was already in place. The plan was efficiently implemented by Vijay Kumar. Mane's death was declared natural and we were safe.

'But then I made four mistakes. One, I sent a congratulatory mail to Ramesh Patel. Secondly, instead of his ID, I clicked on Rao's ID. My third mistake was to tell Patel about it. And my last obvious mistake was to leave the mail regarding the deposit of promised money into my bank undeleted.

'When he came to know that I had sent that mail to Rao, he again felt threatened. He knew Rao was a friend of Mane's and there was a probability that he was aware of the friction between Patel and Mane. He felt Rao would easily put two and two together and come to know that he had got his friend killed. I tried telling him that we should wait and see what action Rao would take, if any, but Patel had made up his mind. He said it was too dangerous to let Rao live. I went along with him because Rao had always been antagonistic towards me, and it had rankled. I had really disliked him for his moralistic posturing.

'Patel felt that Mane's elimination had been perfectly planned, and it could be easily replicated on Rao. We would only have to be careful in choosing a safe place to implement it.'

Kabra again paused to collect his thoughts, and then resumed, 'I had thought I would become chairman of ITL and make some money, but that opportunity was taken away from me. I had no choice but to stick to Patel and do his bidding. I was involved too deeply to pull away. So I agreed to plan out Rao's death. But when you take one wrong step in your life, you continue to slide down and it is difficult to check this downward slide. Right there in my living room where we were discussing these things, the next bit of misfortune struck—our conversation was unfortunately heard by my daughter's tuition teacher who was sitting in a hidden alcove. She was waiting for my daughter to come back from outside. Suddenly there was a rustling sound as she stood up to leave, and we heard her. I went up to her and requested her to go up to my daughter's room to wait.

'Patel again became paranoid that she had overheard everything. I tried to argue with him that I would dismiss her from her services and that she had most probably not understood what we were talking about, but he was firm.

'He told me to find a safe plan to get rid of her. By now I was feeling totally drained out emotionally and had become almost robotic in my obedience to Patel. I had almost burnt my bridges with my previous mentors—Gowri Shankar Prasad and Hansraj Verma. There was also this fear lurking in my mind that they were sure to discover that I was ganging up with their rival, but I refused to confront this at that time. Ramesh Patel was behaving like the head of a banana republic and I had no choice but to continue to obey him.'

'You could have come to the police,' said Ravi.

'And what would have happened? I would have been "eliminated", if not by Patel, then definitely by my former mentors! I had to literally choose between the devil on one side and the deep sea on the other. I decided to carry on with the devil.'

He paused and again continued, 'First we had to handle Rao. All we had to find out was his schedule for the coming month. Arora provided that and also the fact that Rao and his elder son did not like each other; and that they had plans of going to their farmhouse together on 9 and 10 September. Once more, we used low-level employees in need of money for our plan. Arora found them for us. But we had some time to implement Rao's murder as his visit to the farmhouse was a month away so, meanwhile, I concentrated on Rupali.

'Arora again gave us a dossier on her background that revealed that relations with her husband were not good. We used the milkman this time but made it look like her husband was the culprit.'

He took a deep breath before he went on, 'Sunanda was very special to me, and I will not deny that we were having an affair. But innocently she went through the SMSes in my mobile when I was planning Rao's murder and started asking too many questions. I had also taken her along when I recruited Balram Singh, the security guard at the farmhouse, and given him the advance money.

'And again, I had taken her with me when Roop Singh the milkman was given his promised share of money after Rupali's death. We stopped the car at a distance and my driver delivered the money, but unfortunately when he came back he verbally confirmed that he had handed over the money to the person.

'Sunanda again asked me who this person was, but I just laughed and told her not to worry herself about these things; it was just a business deal. But I knew Sunanda was a very smart woman and would put two and two together and could start blackmailing me later. She knew one person's name was Balram, to whom I had given money, and the other person she knew I had paid was Roop Singh. Although she did not know his name, she knew it was just outside the medical college campus and soon after Rupali's death.

'She was slowly becoming a nuisance, prying into my cellphone messages, which could prove dangerous in the future. I should have put an end to the relationship long back but was postponing the decision since she was a very pleasant companion.

'My plan this time was brilliant. I came to know about Shweta's antipathy towards her and it was easy to put the idea into the innocent girl's head.

'Lastly, we were able to carry out Rao's murder. We were sure the son would be blamed, and he was. We were happy that our plan was a success; and I got my second payment.

'Everything seemed to be going smoothly, nobody suspected Mane's death was unnatural. Arvind was arrested for Rupali's murder, Vineet for his father's and I thought no one could connect me to Sunanda's murder. I was also quite sure that no one would come to know that the four murders had a common thread to them. But suddenly you guys were on my trail, how did you latch on?'

Ravi smiled, 'Ramesh Patel threw a lot of red herrings in our path and we were misled into believing it was the board that was responsible for the murders, whereas it was our common "benefactor" who was the main culprit. His moves were worthy of Vishwanathan Anand. He got you to plan the murders and kept himself in the background, and then when he had finished using you, he got us into the picture to nail you. And all along he also made sure that he was destroying the cricket board's reputation—absolutely brilliant! But why did he trust that you would not reveal everything to us?'

'I called him up after you came to question me and he made a pact with me. The pact was that he would deposit 2.5 crore rupees again into my Swiss account if I keep my mouth shut. He said the police would go after the board members and after a while the case would fizzle out. He would also get me the best lawyers and have me out of prison at the earliest, after which I would join his business. I believed him since he is really a very powerful and canny person. But now he has stopped taking my calls and has abandoned me to my fate.'

'Why did you leave the mail from Patel undeleted?'

'I wanted it as a record to confront him with, if the money was not found to have been credited.'

Ravi had heard enough. His expression was grave and his eyes cold. 'Will you sign your confessional statement?'

Rajeev Kabra read it through and quietly added: 'This is my confession, and I am giving this statement of my own free will, without any coercion from anyone.' After signing it he handed it to the DCP.

Ravi had Kabra escorted to his room and walked out—his mind working feverishly.

Nineteen

'Chief, Ramesh Patel has been playing the pied piper with the two of us and Kabra,' Rahul exclaimed. They were sitting in Ravi's office with all the data and evidence spread before them, their pulses racing now that they knew they were close to the end of this case that had been keeping them busy for months.

'Rahul, from hereon we are going to play the pipe and Ramesh Patel will have to follow!'

Ravi rang up Ajay Shukla, 'Hi, this is DCP Ravi and I have a very big lead for your channel, can you come over?'

Shukla was excited, 'I'll be there in half an hour!'

'Rahul, we bring him here and arrest him. Then get everything out of him quickly so we have a solid case against Ramesh Patel.'

Ajay Shukla reached Ravi's office in thirty minutes dot and entered almost running, 'Hello, I can't wait to hear the big news—tell me! And I too have some mindblowing information to reveal.' He was nearly breathless.

'Okay, then you first. You really are a very useful guy to know,' said Ravi wryly.

'Mr Patel has told me to tell you that there has been a major fallout between the two leading men in the board, and there is going to be literally a big bang in the closing ceremony of ITL.'

Ravi's forehead creased, 'Did he clarify?'

'No, those were his words. Now tell me what you have.'

'Ajay, we are going to arrest you as a co-conspirator in the murders of Mane, S.N. Rao and Rupali.'

'WHAT DID YOU SAY?!!!' Ajay nearly fell off his chair.

'You heard me right. You have played a nice game with us for a long time, but we have caught up with you.'

'Guys, believe me, I am totally bewildered at what you are saying,' Ajay looked incredulous.

'You mean to say you have no idea that it is *your channel owner* who is responsible for all the murders?'

'You mean Mr Patel, how is that possible? Please believe me. I have no knowledge at all about what you are insinuating. If he did what you guys say he did, it was without my knowledge. I just acted as he told me, thinking his only aim was to avenge the insults and financial loss he had suffered at the hands of the board.'

'Your boss has been playing a game of chess. If you are telling the truth, the pawns on his board were Rajeev Kabra, you and both of us. Ajay, we will not arrest you at present, but confiscate your mobile and keep you in detention for a couple of days. We do not want you to talk to your boss and reveal what went on here. You will be treated well, but it is for your own good that you remain underground for the present. However, we will inform your family that you are safe.'

Ajay Shukla looked very pale. 'I will cooperate with you guys, since I want my name cleared.'

Ravi called in his inspector and told him to do the needful. When the inspector had taken Ajay away, Ravi turned to Rahul, 'What do you think?'

'Chief, I think Patel is planning something big and by giving us a hint about the fallout between Hansraj Verma and Gowri Prasad, he hopes to pin it on one of them.'

'He thinks he is being very smart, but we will outwit him this time.'

'Chief, I think I know what he will do,' Rahul said thoughtfully. He will get one of them killed. It might be in the closing ceremony this time where security can never be that foolproof. A professional killer can perform this act and easily disappear into the crowd.'

'Okay, let us assume that this is what is being planned and make our countermove.' Ravi looked worried. He rang up the CBI director, 'Sir, we need to see you immediately.'

'Come over, I am in my office.'

When Ravi and Rahul reached there, Ravi updated him. After he'd spoken his senior had something to say, 'Ravi, one question—how do you know Rajeev Kabra is telling the truth? The way this case is going we do not know who is telling the truth, or playing what games!'

Ravi responded, 'I agree sir, but we do have some evidence to prove that he is telling the truth, and in any case we cannot take a chance. If there is even a remote possibility that we can save a life, we have to take steps to do so.'

'Fine, I will go along with you, but if you are proved wrong, you will surrender charge to me in this case.'

Ravi had to agree.

'Rahul,' said Ravi, the finals are about to end, and it will be followed by the closing ceremony. Get a team ready and let's leave for Ferozshah Kotla grounds as soon as the CBI director reaches here. Constable Hassan will drive us there. We'll go in our jeep, and the rest of the police team can follow. Organize things quickly.'

~

In the final lap, the ITL had generated quite a frenzy. The media was going crazy and so was the crowd, especially because the finals were between the home team, the Delhi Darers who were playing against the Kolkata Killers.

Amongst the fifty thousand-odd spectators were two elderly couples, the Iyers and the Sheikhs who had come to watch it live.

'You know Ibrahim, Hema is a new convert to the game,' said Iyer to his new acquaintance. 'She has actually given up her soaps and even religious serials to travel with me from Chennai to watch the T20 finals. We used to live in Delhi before so we are supporting the Delhi Darers.'

Ibrahim Sheikh laughed, 'Rubina is also like your wife. She has decided to follow the game so that the two of us can spend more time together! This is the first time she has travelled outside Kolkata to watch a sporting event live. We will obviously be supporting Kolkata Killers.'

Suddenly there was an excited roar from the crowd as the players walked into the field, and everyone scampered back to their seats.

For over a month, the nation, and half the world, had either watched the tournament 'live' or its highlights, and had been as involved in the league matches as the thirteen players on the ground or the nine sitting in the dugouts with the reserve players.

As for the franchise owners, they too had given up their money-making ventures to be 'one with the boys'. Not that they didn't expect to make money out of these matches. In fact, many of them were physically present, but mentally plotting how to generate more wealth out of their latest acquisition!

Now the finals had begun and the excitement was tremendous. Kolkata Killers had won the toss and had elected to field.

Ibrahim was elated, 'This is a good omen. I have a feeling we are going to win the tournament.'

'Ibrahim, you were the underdogs and have come this far, but I think your luck is about to run out. We have a very determined captain, who hates to lose!' was Srini Iyer's retort.

'If your captain is determined, ours is more so. He has managed to enthuse the players to become a fighting bunch, and I think they are on an unbeatable winning streak.'

'Let's see who turns out to be right,' Srini responded and they turned their attention to the match.

Delhi Darers batted well but did not get the score of 180 plus that they were aiming for. They made 150 for the loss of 5 wickets in twenty overs, which worked out to an average of 7.5 runs per over. It was not unachievable.

Now it was the turn of Kolkata Killers. Their approach was cautious since it was the final and the stakes were high. So in the end they prevailed and lifted the trophy. They made 151 for the loss of 7 wickets in twenty overs and won the tournament. They had been the lowest-rated team when the tournament had begun, but had fought and clawed their way up the league matches to reach the top.

Ibrahim was jubilant and even Rubina was jumping up and down with joy, 'We did it! We did it!'

Iyer and Hema hugged both of them. 'You must both come to Chennai for a visit. We will show you around,' they said.

'And Kolkata is also a tourist's delight. Please give us an opportunity to entertain you. We are very hospitable people besides being the winners tonight!' said Ibrahim, his eyes twinkling.

The tournament had exactly the fairy tale ending that the board had wanted. Slam-bang? Gully? Call it what you will, but it was a huge success. All the doubting Thomases were silenced. But the excitement generated was not only due to the matches. What transpired during the closing ceremony provided enough thrills to last many people a lifetime.

The three officers along with a team of men were on their way to Ferozshah Kotla grounds. They had to reach before the ceremony got over and it had already begun according to the news on their jeep radio. A running commentary was describing the scintillating events on the ground. It had begun with a specially composed song by India's leading music director, and was followed by dance numbers by two leading actresses. The last item was a laser display depicting India's history that was continuously applauded by the thrilled spectators. But the three officers, their adrenaline pumping, hardly listened to the commentary. They had a deadline to meet and a possible crime to prevent.

Ravi turned to his driver, 'Hassan, drive fast and for a change keep the sirens on, we need to reach there as soon as we can!'

It should have taken them only half an hour to reach the cricket ground. But the metro rail construction forced them into a long detour and it took them twenty minutes more to cover the extra distance. This was in spite of the fact that their best driver was at the wheel.

'How much further now Hassan?' asked Ravi anxiously. They just *had* to reach before the ceremony ended!

'Sahib, we've almost reached the signal near the ground and from there it is just a ten-minute drive.'

But at the signal they were shocked when they were stopped from proceeding further by a posse of police. Some VIP's arrival was expected!

Ravi quickly got down to show his credentials, but just then a cavalcade of a visiting foreign dignitary roared past them and they had to wait. They were going to be too late!

Ravi jumped back into the jeep and turned to the driver, 'Faster Hassan!'

'Don't worry sahib, there's a side road that I can take. We will reach quickly.'

They zoomed through the side lane as Hassan expertly manoeuvred the vehicle through a small village-like colony. Hassan stopped the jeep outside the stadium with a screech and the three officers jumped out. They showed their credentials and forced their way into the VIP box where the board members and their families were seated. The last of the firecrackers and laser show were lighting up the twilight sky as the uniformed men arrived.

'Sir, we have to spread out and look out for any likely suspect around the VIP box!'

Ravi, Rahul and the CBI director surrounded the VIP box. The local security head had noticed them. He came over wanting to know what was happening. Ravi told him that they were there to prevent a crime, he could join them in their vigil but not involve the rest of his men, to avoid any confusion.

Just as the spectacular show ended, the master of ceremonies came to the mike.

'Good evening ladies and gentlemen,' his voice boomed, 'We have reached the end of the show. It has been an evening that I am sure all of us have enjoyed tremendously. ITL has been a huge success and the two men mainly responsible for it will address you now. Ladies and gentlemen, first I present Mr Manik Jindal, the ITL chairman!'

Jindal came briskly to the podium, 'Ladies and gentlemen, the last four months, since we decided to launch ITL, have been like a roller-coaster ride for all of us in the cricket board. It has been a joint effort by all the members of the board and I am only the face of ITL. I would like to therefore thank all of them, and especially Mr Gowri Prasad and Mr Hansraj Verma for backing me completely. Next I would like to thank the dynamic team which has worked tirelessly with me to ensure a smooth running of the tournament. It has been a stupendous task and they have performed it well. I would like to announce that I will retain the same team for future tournaments. Ladies and gentlemen, a big round of applause for them!' Thunderous applause followed.

There was no mention of Rajeev Kabra, the man who had worked the hardest but was now in custody.

Jindal resumed, 'I would also like to thank all our sponsors for believing in us, and last but not the least, you the audience in the stadium and all the TV viewers in the country and around the world—thank you for making ITL a success! Please continue to support us in the future!'

After the applause had died down, the master of ceremonies was back. 'Ladies and gentlemen, I give you the cricket board president, Shri Gowri Shankar Prasad!'

There was a huge cheer as the president took the mike, 'Thank you friends, the success of ITL would not have been possible without all of you. It has been a great day for Indian cricket and I am sure we are going to reach undreamt of heights in the next few years. All the members of the cricket board have worked very hard to make this tournament a success but I would like to make a special mention of Mr Manik Jindal. I will also like to thank all the players who have come from different countries but have gelled so well together with their Indian team members, and also the various associations for granting them the permission to participate in the tournament. After the present board has taken over, Indian cricket has done terrifically and I promise you we will continue to do so. Recently, there has been some bad publicity involving the board, but let me assure you that we are totally in the clear. We will make sure . . .'

Suddenly there was a loud explosion that was heard not only by the whole crowd but also the millions of viewers in the country and around the world. There was total confusion in the VIP box. The crowd was shocked! Was it a terrorist attack, what should they do? Panic had nearly set in ...

Ravi's eyes had not left the VIP box even for a second when the board president had been giving his speech. And just as he was ending, Ravi spotted the movement he was looking out for. He fired instantly and also ran into the box. There were two gunshots, one from Ravi's pistol and another which was directed at Gowri Shankar Prasad but got deflected safely because Ravi had aimed at the gunman's shoulder. Immediately, security men surrounded the VIP box. The gunman who had fired and was injured by Ravi was Gowri Shankar's own personal security guard!

'Quick, get him into an ambulance and rush him to the All India,' Ravi told Rahul. 'We must save him and get a statement out of him.'

He then turned to the CBI director who had picked up the security man's gun with his kerchief and put it safely into his pocket. 'Sir, I think it is time you addressed the crowd to ensure there is no panic, the local security can handle things here. I am going to head to Ramesh Patel's house to arrest him.'

Rahul handcuffed the injured security man and rushed him to the hospital, where he was lucky enough to record his statement before he was taken in for surgery to remove the bullet from his right shoulder.

The CBI director, together with the security on the grounds, was able to keep the crowd from going into a panic.

The crowd finally sat down again and a major pandemonium was averted. The VIPs were safely escorted out before the crowd was allowed to leave in an orderly fashion.

Meanwhile, Ravi took his inspector in his jeep and asked Hassan to drive them to Ramesh Patel's house. They were out of the venue before the crowd started pouring out and the streets were relatively empty, so they were able to move fast. Ravi thought that hopefully the media would not have been told yet about exactly what transpired in the VIP box. Ramesh Patel should be at home, anxiously watching TV and they should be able to catch him there.

Ravi reached Patel's house in twenty minutes and barged in. The security guard at the gate tried to stop him, but withdrew on seeing who it was. But he would certainly try to phone his boss, thought Ravi. So he told Hassan to handle him and ran to the main door of the house with the inspector. The door was opened by a servant and the two officers rushed in.

The sound of heavy police boots alerted the family members who came down to see what the commotion was all about. Luckily, the TV magnate was also one of them. Ravi ran up to Ramesh Patel and handcuffed him. 'I am arresting you for the murders of Sunil Mane, S.N. Rao and Rupali Agarwal, as also for the attempted murder of Shri Gowri Shankar Prasad,' he announced.

Ramesh Patel surrendered quietly without any argument and walked with Ravi to the jeep even as his stunned family members looked on.

Twenty

A court case was soon underway and the hearings went on for nearly two years, during each of which either Ravi or Rahul was personally present when required. In spite of the confessional statements, the evidence gathered had to be submitted in court. There were many ups and downs with witnesses turning hostile, but ultimately a clear and unambiguous verdict was given.

The first to be sentenced was Sanjay. During interrogation in the court, he finally revealed what had happened that night. Neela's evidence, the washed pyjamas, and the statements of other witnesses helped the public prosecutor to break him down. But he sprang a surprise in the court—he said that the evening before Shweta's death he had received an anonymous call and the voice told him that it was Shweta who had pushed Sunanda down the stairs. The person also revealed that he knew everything about Sanjay and his debts and could help out if he eliminated Shweta.

Sanjay had been absolutely livid. Till then he had thought that Sunanda's death was an accident, and when he found out the truth, he could not control himself. Unfortunately, the call had come on the landline in his clinic and could not be traced. But Sanjay was hardly interested in money at that time. All he could think of was to confront Shweta and take revenge!

That night he had woken up at 1.30 p.m. and gone to Shweta's room. He knew she watched TV late into the night. He had taken a glass of hot milk into which he had added lethal doses of her powdered medication. He pretended that he had come up to spend time with her as he could not get sleep. He handed her the milk and told her to drink it as they talked. He casually asked her if she had pushed Sunanda down the stairs and she innocently told him that she had, and why she had done so. She even gave him graphic details.

Shweta was so happy to be with Sanjay that she hardly realized what she was saying or drinking, but suddenly she vomited violently and tossed about all over the room before falling unconscious on the ground. She uprooted her banyan bonsai and died clutching it in her hand.

Sanjay had also come prepared with some injections which he would have given Shweta if the oral dose had failed but there was no need. He was glad she was dead, and had absolutely no remorse, for she had killed his beloved Sunanda. He had then brought a towel to try and clean up some of the mess and then rolled it up along with his night suit that had also got soiled. After getting into a fresh pair of pyjamas, he went to bed again, glad that Neela was sleeping soundly, apparently under the effect of the sedative she had been taking.

Sanjay was convicted for a period of ten years for Shweta's murder. He also divorced Neela on her request.

Vijay Kumar was convicted for Mane's murder and also handed a ten-year term.

Ramu and Balram Singh were sentenced to four years each and Roop Singh to ten years for their role in the Rao and Rupali murders respectively.

Rajeev Kabra was convicted as one of the chief conspirators in all four murders and given a fourteen-year sentence, which was reduced to ten years because he had cooperated with the police in getting the main culprit booked.

Ramesh Patel received a life sentence for his role as the one who planned all the murders.

All the convictions have been challenged and their appeals are pending in the High Court.

The government is said to be investigating the charges of money being pumped in by the board into a major political party.

~

Ravi and Rahul got together once again on a Sunday at the former's house. They were expecting visitors.

'It's over, chief, at least our role in it. My only grouse is that after the hard work we put in, you let the CBI take all the credit.'

'Never mind Rahul, all the people that matter know the truth and anyway our main aim was to get the culprits convicted, which we did.'

'You read a lot of books on psychology, chief, is it so easy to decide to murder so many people?'

'Rahul, Ramesh Patel is a very powerful man who was rendered two severe body blows by fate. First, Sunil Mane borrowed a huge amount from him and refused to pay it back. And Kabra mentioned that Mane had pledged a big property in Mumbai to Patel against this loan, so acquiring that property could also have been an incentive to get rid of the former board treasurer. Then TLI was launched in which he was the chief sponsor and it was derailed by the cricket board. People in his position have large egos. Loss of face and prestige must have mattered to him even more than the heavy financial loss he had sustained. His first and, actually, only intended victim was Mane, supposedly a good friend turned foe; the rest were unlucky victims of chance. The masterstroke was using Ajay Shukla as a decoy to pin the murders on the cricket board. He saw it as a chance to avenge the humiliation he had suffered at their hands.

'This brought us into the picture and Patel kept leading us through a blind alley till we ultimately saw the light.'

'Two things have bothered me chief—one is the money given to Balram the security guard—why were new notes that could be easily traced handed over? Veterans like them should have known better! And secondly, why did Rajeev Kabra go personally to meet all his recruits? He could have sent someone else.'

'Rahul, the new bundle of notes surprised me too. Maybe Rajeev Kabra was short of time and picked up whatever was available, or he was overconfident that they would never be caught. His going personally to meet the people to be used for the crimes was probably because they did not want to trust anybody else with highly "delicate" tasks like this. And also, I am sure they thought that none of the crimes would be discovered as unnatural, leave alone be traced to them except Rupali's, which was obvious, but her husband would have been blamed for it. Remember, the Prime Minister set off the whole investigation because he was not happy that his friend and colleague, S.N. Rao had died suddenly at a remote location, and he wanted to be absolutely sure there was no foul play. If he had not done so, we might never have come into the picture and they may have escaped justice!'

'And also, chief, why do you think Gowri Shankar Prasad met Vineet, and that too in such a secretive manner?'

'I think he was trying to get Vineet to collect some dirt on his father, which he could then use to oust Rao from the board.'

Just then the doorbell rang and Rahul got up to open it, but was beaten to it by Ravi's wife.

It was Dilip, Indu and Anu. Indu came forward and warmly held Ravi's and then Rahul's hands, 'Thank you both, I'm at peace now. The people behind my husband's death have been punished and Vineet has also been exonerated. There is already a positive change in him which we hope will be permanent. And I also want to congratulate you on getting married. We've brought you a small gift which we hope you will not decline.'

'Thank you ma'am! We only did our duty,' saying so Ravi turned to his wife, 'I think the gift is for you.'

Dilip also came forward with his hands extended, 'Super job, sleuths! Both in solving the case and in the choice of wife. We're here to give you another bit of news. We've started a charitable foundation named after my father-in-law in which we want both you and Rahul as honorary trustees, if your department permits.'

'That's great! Thank you!' said both in unison.

'Although about your proposal,' said Ravi, 'we'll find out if we are permitted to become trustees while in active service. I don't think it is possible, but if allowed we'll be delighted to accept. In any case, if you want to help through your new foundation, please do what you can for Roop Singh's wife.'

'Anu will go personally to meet her and will see how to help her. Once again, stupendous job guys!'

After Rao's family had left they continued their reminiscing.

'Chief, Dr Arvind Agarwal came to meet me. He wanted to thank us for bringing out the truth. He also felt that he deserved every bit of misfortune that has come his way for how he treated Rupali. He has been released from prison but his professional life and reputation have been ruined. He has quit his job in the college, and his girlfriend has deserted him. He also continues to remain at loggerheads with his father who supports him financially but treats him very badly.'

'Rahul, I think I agree with him that he got what he deserved. But if it helps in turning his life around like it has done in Vineet's case, something good would still have come out of it.

'Dilip himself has decided to quit the board and join hands with Surya to revive the TLI. They have good sponsors and this time round, they think it will be a huge success.'

'And chief, I hear the ITL's league matches are to be held again for the third time. I'm sure *their* coffers will continue to overflow.'

'Yes, there have also been fresh elections in the board and new members have come in. Hansraj Verma and Manik Jindal have been defeated. Rahul, there was an article in the *Times* by Vikram Dutt that the future of Indian cricket is very bright. That may be true, but I think the power games will continue. Verma and Jindal will continue to pull strings from outside the board, and Rajeev Kabra from inside the prison. And what Ramesh Patel will do, no one knows! Also, as the TLI is being revived, there is every likelihood that there will be friction again with the official league.'

Neela smiled and summed up succinctly, 'Old board against new, TLI versus ITL—the games will certainly carry on!'

She had been following the story avidly ever since she had married Ravi and was proud and happy that the case had been brought to a satisfactory conclusion by Rahul and her husband.

Acknowledgements

I am grateful to my mother, who is the fountainhead of any talent I possess.

A warm thanks to my husband and son, the two Dr Sundararajans in my life who have painstakingly performed the arduous task of the 'logical' editing of this book.

I am also very grateful to Geetha V., Jayanthi Srinivasan, Shanth Mannige, my brother Rajesh, my nephew Venkat and my niece Aparna, for reading the manuscript and providing incisive and encouraging feedback.

I must not forget to mention my brother-in-law Govindan for stripping me of my complacency and making me work harder.

Very special thanks to Padma Bhushan Shri Chandu Borde, former test cricketer and chairman of the national selection committee, for reviewing the book from a cricketer's perspective and giving a very kind review.

An equally special thanks to former Commissioner of Police, Pune, Mr P.S. Narayanaswami for reviewing the book with a policeman's perspective and for his appreciative comments.

Vaishali Mathur and the rest of the Penguin editorial team for their invaluable help at every step, and to all my friends and patients who believe in me.